# A TIME TO CHOOSE

# A TIME TO CHOOSE

martha attema

ORCA BOOK PUBLISHERS

Canadian Cataloguing in Publication Data
Attema, Martha, 1949–
  A time to choose

  ISBN 1-55143-045-2
  I. Title.
PS8551.T73T55 1995    jC813'.54    C95-910446-1    PZ7.A77Ti
1995

Publication assistance provided by The Canada Council
Cover design by Christine Toller
Cover painting by Imagecraft Studio Ltd.

Printed and bound in Canada

Orca Book Publishers
PO Box 5626, Station B
Victoria, BC   V8R 6S4
Canada

Orca Book Publishers
PO Box 468
Custer, WA   98240-0468
USA

10   9   8   7   6   5   4   3   2   1

To all the sons, daughters and grandchildren of former *NSB* Party members who to this day live with guilt and unanswered questions.

# Acknowledgements

The following people need to be acknowledged, for without their assistance this book would not have been possible.

Margaret Geurtsen-Dekker and others who shared their war stories and experiences with me.

Jaitsche Wassenaar's book *It Pak Fan Us Heit* (*My Father's Suit*), which inspired me to write the story.

Marla J. Hayes, Wendy Champaign and Bea Mooney for their patience, editorial suggestions and moral support.

The North Bay Children's Writers group and Ruth Ward for their support and suggestions.

Heinz and Helga Schleuting for correcting my usage of the German language.

Donna Sinclair for inspiring me to write from my shadow.

My sister-in-law, for researching libraries and mailing and faxing materials from the Netherlands.

My sister-in-law's mother, who wrote about the people and their everyday struggles during the Second World War in her beautiful handwriting.

Albert Attema for his support and for making sure the historical facts were correct.

Romkje, Sjoerd and Rikst Attema for their suggestions and corrections.

And Ann Featherstone, children's book editor at Orca. Working with Ann has been a rewarding learning experience. Ann's understanding of my needs, her hard work and invaluable editing suggestions have helped bring my creative ideas to print.

# Table of Contents

# <u>August 1944</u>

Howling sirens pierced the stillness of the night.

"Damn!" Sixteen-year-old Johannes van der Meer was startled out of a deep sleep. He stumbled out of bed and groped around in the darkened bedroom for his clothes. The blackout curtains, which covered his bedroom window, made it difficult for him to find his socks. He heard his sister Anneke stumble in the next room.

"Johannes! Anneke! Hurry!" his mother urged from the bottom of the stairs.

"Wait for me, Johannes!" his ten-year-old sister called. He stopped at the top of the stairs. Together they found their way down.

Holding a small oil lamp, Mother stood in the hallway. "Let's go." She moved her arm in the direction of the kitchen. The light from the lamp danced ahead as they hurried into the shelter.

Settling down, they heard the droning of the English planes. Good, Johannes nodded, the Allied Lancasters were on their way to Germany. The air base near the town of Leeuwarden had also been their target for the last few nights. Only five kilometres away from their farm, this base was used by the Germans for their nightly attacks on Allied planes. Anti-aircraft guns were hidden in man-made hills covered with soil, grass and bushes. Rumor had it the shelters were filled with bombs and explosives. If these hills were bombed, the whole area within a radius of two kilometres would be destroyed. Johannes shivered. He didn't want to think about that possibility.

The concrete floor of the shelter cooled his feet even through the socks he had managed to find underneath his bed. He flopped down on the wooden bench beside Anneke. Their shelter was a small concrete space behind the laundry room. A steel door sealed the room against outside enemies.

"Where's Father?" Johannes shouted as his mother closed the heavy door. The engines of the airplanes and the sound of the anti-aircraft guns made it almost impossible for them to hear one another.

"I don't know," his mother answered. "He should be home soon." She put the oil lamp on the floor in the centre of the room and sat down on the bench. Anneke snuggled close to her mother. Johannes saw the fear in his sister's eyes. Mother's face was drawn. She wore a blue wool cardigan over her cotton nightgown. Her wavy hair, which was held back with two side combs during the day, hung forward, concealing her eyes.

"Did the Germans pick him up or . . . "

The steel door opened and Johannes' father stomped in. "It's bad out there," he said. He unbuttoned his black uniform jacket and sat down across from Johannes.

"Where were you, Father?"

"Oh, I had to check out some places, Johannes." His father bent to fumble with his bootlaces.

"What places? Where? Who was with you?" Johannes

rose from the bench, his fists clenched.

"Johannes! I do not have to answer to . . . "

"Stop it! Both of you!" Mother stood up. "Johannes, sit down! You do not talk to your father like that." She paced back and forth in the small space. "There's enough war above our heads." She jabbed her finger at the ceiling.

Silence fell upon the family while above the air battle continued. Johannes listened. Over the last four years he'd learned to recognize the sounds of the different planes. The Lancasters made the droning sound. Now he heard the screaming of German Messerschmidts, the ones with shark teeth painted on their noses. He'd seen them fly over low, many times. The sharp ra-ta-ta-ta of anti-aircraft guns and the staccato sound of the cannons made him shiver. He crossed his legs and pressed his palms against the bench. He tensed the muscles in his arms. His heart pounded in rhythm with the attacks. Anneke clung to her mother. Father held his head in his hands.

Johannes closed his eyes. In the beginning of the war he had been fascinated by the aircraft, German as well as Allied. Sometime during the summer of 1941, the R.A.F. bombers began flying over Friesland during the night, attacking military targets in Germany. The first bombers were called Blenheims. These planes were slow and needed to fly low, which made them an easy target for the German night fighters and *FLAK, Flieger Abwehr Kanonen* (anti-aircraft guns). The attacks hadn't been as frequent then. The Lancasters that were used now were better planes. They carried more bombs and attacked their targets with greater accuracy. Johannes sighed and rubbed his forehead. Unfortunately, many Allied plane crews were buried in Friesian soil.

Lately the air raids had become routine. Three, four nights a week the family rushed down to the shelter. At the beginning of the war Johannes had been very excited during the air attacks, as he believed the Germans would soon be defeated. Now he was often annoyed to have his sleep interrupted, although he couldn't shake the fear that their farm would be hit. Too many bombs had missed their target and had destroyed the homes of innocent people in the area.

A boom like thunder shook the earth. The building trembled.

Johannes sat up with a jolt.

"That was a big one," Father said.

"I hope it didn't hit any homes," his mother responded, her bottom lip trembling.

"I hope they flattened the whole air base," Johannes declared in a loud voice.

"Johannes!" His father shot a sharp glance at him, a deep frown creasing his forehead. Johannes bowed his head and said nothing.

An hour later, after the "all clear" *to-o-o-t*, the night became silent once more. The Allied planes must have flown back to their bases in England. The van der Meer family returned to their sleeping quarters.

In his room Johannes tossed and turned for several hours. Finally he stopped trying to sleep. Just before dawn he dressed in his dark blue coveralls, grabbed his cap and without a sound left the house. When he walked past the barn, Bijke, the family's old black and white dog, didn't even wake up. Johannes' long legs, heavy with fatigue, took him to his favourite thinking spot, the gate to their pastures.

He climbed on top of the gate and sat on the wooden bar. A blanket of early morning mist lifted from Friesland's farmland. One by one the large bodies of his father's cows lumbered into view. Johannes stretched and yawned. In another hour his father and Douwe the old farm hand would arrive and disturb the peace with much clanging of the milk pails and cans.

"Peace," he sighed. As far as his eyes could see, the

land looked peaceful. The contours of neighbouring farms and villages came slowly into view through the mist. Church steeples, untouched by this night's raid, stood proud as beacons in the flat landscape. The tranquility at this hour was deceiving, Johannes thought. Long ago, there was a time when he'd taken peace for granted.

He was only twelve then, but Johannes remembered clearly the radio announcer's words: "Today, in the early morning of the tenth of May, 1940, German troops attacked the Netherlands."

Father had clapped him on the shoulder. "You'll see, Johannes, from now on things can only get better. Look at Germany's economy — it's flourishing. This is the end of the great depression."

All day Johannes had listened to the radio. He'd heard that the German troops not only had invaded his country, but Belgium and France as well.

Two days later, the Nazis entered the province of Friesland, and by the evening of the twelfth of May, all of Friesland had been occupied. The Dutch Army fought bravely and the Germans, who had expected to take all of the Netherlands in a day, lost heavily, especially in Friesland.

Then came the German revenge. They bombed and nearly destroyed the entire seaport of Rotterdam, causing devastation among the Dutch people.

Mother had been distraught. "Do you still think things will get better?" she had glared at Father. That was the first time Johannes observed tension in his parents' relationship.

When the Germans threatened the destruction of other major cities, like Amsterdam and The Hague, the Dutch Army had had no choice but to capitulate on May the fifteenth.

The Dutch royal family and the government fled to England. When the Germans threatened to invade England, Princess Juliana and the two little princesses escaped to

Canada. Queen Wilhelmina and her son-in-law, Prince Bernhard, stayed in Britain so she could support and encourage her people by talking to them on the illegal English radio station.

In the beginning, the van der Meers hadn't noticed too much of the war. After the capitulation life had resumed much as before, and the Germans kept their promise of paying the farmers well. The small air base near the city of Leeuwarden was extended with new runways. Several hundred people found employment and were paid well. After the years of unemployment, the income was a welcome change for many families in the area. But as the war continued, the Germans forced people into labour with no pay.

At that time it hadn't bothered Johannes that his father was a member of the National Socialist Movement, the only political party allowed under German occupation. Modelled after the German Nazi Party, the organization was run by Dutch ministers, but was completely under German control. At first many believed that a better economy would solve the country's problems. As a result, most farmers became members of the National Socialist Movement. There were real benefits. The Germans paid good money for dairy and grain products. Uncle Jan, father's older brother, always said, "Hitler pays more for our products than the Queen ever did." Uncle Jan was a faithful party member.

But as time passed and the war showed no sign of ending, people began to realize that the Germans were not all that reliable. For one thing, they paid with money that was worthless. Now the benefits were not so clear. Many farmers terminated their memberships in the Movement.

Johannes wished his father had given up his membership and joined the resistance. At first he hadn't seen his father as a traitor. But in the last two years Johannes had begun to worry. More and more people were working in the resistance. Now he often wondered if his father was an informer.

Johannes shook his head. He wanted to treasure this morning's silence for a little while longer. He stared at the herd in front of him. Up in the sky, a lark sang. The rising sun seemed naive and innocent, as if nothing had happened during the night. His wooden shoe kicked one of the gate planks. "This goddamn war! When will it end?" he grunted.

"Johannes! Is that you out there?"

He jumped down. "Yes, Father. I'm coming!"

"Round them up, Johannes," his father yelled. "Douwe and I will meet you in ten minutes."

Johannes' eyes lingered on their farm. The high barn with the stables at the front dominated the scene. The white-plastered living quarters were attached to the main building by a low section which contained the large kitchen and a hallway. This part looked like the neck between the main body — the stables and barn — and the head — the living quarters. High poplar trees protected the building from northwestern storms. At the far end the apple trees stood sheltered by a long row of ash trees. Linden trees gave the front of the house an air of majesty. In the summer their crowns of lime-green leaves formed a canopy which concealed the farm entrance from the main road.

He felt proud of their farm. One day it would all belong to him. Father had told him this many times. A shadow crossed his face. Would it ever belong to him and . . . Sietske? Would he and Sietske live on the farm during a peaceful time? Would they have a family some day?

"Hey, Johannes! Are you sleeping? Get the ladies up! We're coming!"

With a jolt Johannes opened the gate. The put-put of the old tractor filled the bright morning air. Father drove the tractor; the wagon hitched behind it carried Douwe, his loyal and only farm hand. Two years ago his father had two more farm hands, but they'd chosen to leave and work for a farmer who didn't belong to the National Socialist Movement.

Johannes trotted to the far end of the meadow where a few cows had found a place to rest after the sirens had stopped. "Hey! Come on! Time for milking!" he called.

The tractor and wagon arrived as he rounded up the last cows. In a fenced-in area they tied the cows to the wagon.

Johannes watched Father walk over to Bertha, his favourite cow. His eyes followed the movements of the tall, slim man with the same straight brown hair as his own. People told Johannes he looked like his father. They had the same high foreheads, same blue eyes and perfectly straight noses. The only visible difference was that his father wore black-rimmed glasses. Father was a proud man. His thin lips made his expression stern, even when talking to the cows. He scratched the animal behind the horns.

Johannes had always respected his father. But lately he had so many questions. How was it possible for this kind and gentle man to collaborate with a ruthless enemy? Lately Johannes' thoughts ran in circles. Sometimes he felt anger toward his father, like last night in the shelter. Sometimes he hated him. Then, at moments like this, while watching him with the animals, he felt opposite emotions. Johannes shrugged his shoulders and walked up to the cow called Maaike, who was waiting to be milked.

Slowly, Douwe, his work clothes patched and worn, walked over to a second cow. Douwe seemed stiff this morning. He breathed unevenly as he crouched down on the three-legged milking stool beside the cow. Johannes watched him lean against the cow's stomach. Douwe and his wife, Pietsje, lived in the small house at the end of the farm's driveway, close to the main road.

"Are you all right, Douwe?" Johannes sat on a stool next to Maaike.

"Yes, I think so. It's my wife, you know. She's scared to death of the air raids. Every night when the sirens go off she wants us to hide in the kitchen cabinets, under the counter."

"The kitchen cabinets?" Johannes stopped milking. He turned to stare at the older man.

"Yes, it's true. Every night she pushes herself inside one of those darn cabinets and wants me to do the same thing. Until last night I was able to avoid it. Usually I help her inside and close the door. Then I go back to bed. I figure if a bomb hits our house, I might as well die a comfortable death in my own bed. But last night she made me go in first and closed the door. She thinks the granite countertop will save us. I will not go in there again. I'm stiff as a board. My whole body aches."

Johannes shook with laughter. He rolled off the stool into the grass and laughed so hard his stomach hurt. "I'm sorry, Douwe. The way you described it, it was like a movie playing before my eyes."

"Yes, I guess it must have been a funny sight." Douwe smiled as he patted his cow gently.

Johannes returned to his chores. Early morning sounds accompanied the rhythm of the milk spraying into the metal pail. In the distance, the sound of a truck disturbed the peace. A military truck, he thought.

The bastards were up early, too.

# Sietske

His bike screeched as Johannes pedalled down the lane to the main road. The rubber on the steel tires was almost completely worn off. It was impossible to find material to cover tires these days. Like everything else he used to take for granted before the war, rubber tires were no longer available. A good bike was a luxury. Every boy dreamed about owning a bike with air-filled tires.

Johannes whistled. It took a lot of energy to turn the pedals, but he was in good shape, even though he no longer rode the ten kilometres into town each day to attend the College of Agriculture. Two years ago the administration had closed the school. When so many farm hands had been forced to work in the weapons factories in Germany, most of the students were needed on the farms. His father had also needed Johannes when two of their three labourers left.

He crossed the road and turned right. Father wanted him to pick up the shaft for one of their wheelbarrows. Theirs had broken in half and needed to be welded by the blacksmith who lived on the south side of the village. On the way in he would check on Minne, his best friend.

Few cars travelled the roads these days. Most people had to turn in their cars to the Germans, and gas was hard to get. His father still had some fuel, enough to let the old tractor run, although Johannes had no idea where he got it.

He passed several farms on the way. The weather was still warm, which was a bit unusual for the middle of September. At least they had harvested enough hay to feed their cows during the winter.

From the village another bicyclist approached him. Even as the figure moved closer with every turning pedal, Johannes couldn't make out if it was a man or a woman. The rider came closer. Johannes' heart pounded in his chest. He recognized Sietske! He waved. She hesitated and then her hand left the handlebars to return his greeting. His smile touched his ears. Even though Sietske lived on a neighbouring farm, Johannes hadn't seen her for three weeks.

The two riders both stopped at the same time. Her eyes were a warm brown and dark curls framed her oval face. A crimson red coloured her cheeks.

"You're back," he whispered.

She just nodded. Sietske wore a faded blue skirt and a blouse that bore bold prints of trains and locomotives. She followed his gaze. "Mother and I made this out of the old curtains that used to hang in my brothers' room when they were little," she smiled. "Where did you get your shirt?"

"I inherited this from Grandfather van der Meer. Grandmother saved all his clothes after he died, and now they come in handy," he returned the smile. "How was it at your aunt's?"

"Boring," she laughed.

"I missed you," he said softly.

"I missed you too, Johannes." Her face grew serious. "I shouldn't be seen with you. My father will send me away again. I don't want to go."

"I know," he said. He grabbed her hand. "Meet me tonight at ten under the bridge."

"I can't promise anything, Johannes. My parents are keeping a close eye on me. They watch every move I make. The reason I was allowed to bike into town today is because Bauke is in . . . " She stopped and looked away.

"What happened to your brother?" he asked.

"I can't tell you."

He swallowed. "You can't or you won't?"

"I can't," she whispered.

"You don't trust me. Just like the rest of your family," he said bitterly. "And all because of my father's membership in the party." He took his hand away and thrust it in his pocket. A shadow crossed the road. Johannes shivered and looked up to see just a single cloud in the clear sky.

Sietske stood beside her bike. The top of her head barely reached his shoulder. A lock of brown, curly hair lay damp on her forehead. Both hands remained on the handlebars. She pressed her lips into a thin line and her eyes, now cold, stared at him.

He coughed and moved his bike away from her. "I have to go. You're right. We'd better not be seen together." With one leap he jumped on his bike and pedalled away with all his might. Without looking back once, he drove straight into the village.

As he passed the school, three little boys ran in front of him. They jumped to the side and turned to look at him.

"Hi, Johannes!" one of them called.

"Hi, boys," he answered.

"He's a collaborator," he heard one of them say.

"No," the first one answered. "Johannes isn't a collaborator. His father is. Johannes is nice."

"Damn!" He pedalled harder. "Johannes is nice," he repeated out loud. He laughed.

What about his father?

Minne's house was on the outskirts of the village. The corner house was part of a row of houses that belonged to the church. The surrounding grounds and farms, located south of the village, had provided jobs for many villagers for hundreds of years.

His friend's mother answered the door. Tall and slim, she had strawberry blond hair that normally was combed away from her face, but was now in disarray.

"Minne isn't home," she said, wiping her eyes on her apron, her thin face swollen from crying.

"Did something happen to your husband?" he asked. "Or to Minne?"

"No. No. Everything is okay. Bye, Johannes. Come back another time." She closed the door on him.

Slowly Johannes biked down to the blacksmith's. Something must have happened at Minne's house. The soft-spoken woman had always been kind to him. Now he had noticed a distance in her eyes — rejection.

Johannes always visited Minne on Sunday afternoons. During the last few years the two friends had spent most of those afternoons fishing, bicycling, playing cards with Minne's father or going skating during the winter. When they were small, Minne's father had taught them where and how to catch the biggest fish. He'd helped them make their first kite. Now Minne's father worked in Germany, in one of the many weapons factories.

Johannes hoped there wouldn't be too many people in the shop. Although the blacksmith was still polite, Johannes didn't feel like talking today or listening to others' comments about his father. It wasn't his fault his father collaborated with the Germans. But why hadn't his father joined the resistance like Sietske's family?

"You came to pick up the shaft?" The smith stood in the doorway of the shop. A big, burly man with lots of grey-brown hair greeted him. His worn and greasy work clothes were in dire need of a good scrubbing, but soap was hard to get these days.

"It's fixed, Johannes. It's time this damn war was over, so we can buy decent materials and new equipment." The blacksmith spit a wad of tobacco on the street in front of him. "Your father must be starting to worry now that British and Canadian troops have freed the southern parts of the Netherlands."

Johannes didn't answer. He hadn't noticed his father's fears, although lately he seemed more quiet.

"The Allies are moving quickly to Arnhem and Grave. It's only a matter of time now. As soon as they cross the rivers, Johannes, this war will be over." Another wad of tobacco landed close to Johannes' wooden shoes. "I can see you're not well informed. The German radio announcers keep this information hidden from their loyal listeners."

Johannes nodded. At home they listened only to the German station on the radio, which his father had hidden underneath the floor of the pantry. Even though it was forbidden for everybody, even party members, to keep radios, he knew that most people had their radios hidden and secretly listened to the British station, the BBC.

The blacksmith walked into the shop and took out the shaft. "I'll tie it onto the back of your bike," he said as he pulled a dirty piece of rope out of his pocket. "All right. I'll add it to your father's credit in my books. Off you go. Your father can pay me after the war, when money is worth more."

Johannes took a parcel out of his saddlebags and handed it to the older man. "Compliments from my mother," he said.

"Your mother makes the best butter in the area, Johannes." The blacksmith's laugh echoed in the street as Johannes turned the corner.

On the way home, Johannes thought about his conversation with Sietske. How could he have been so stupid? She didn't trust him. No, that wasn't true. She did trust him. In his heart he knew she did. She was torn between the pressure her family put on her not to see him anymore and their friendship. Friendship? No. Lately, it was something else.

Since grade one, Sietske and Johannes had biked the two kilometres to school together. All through their school years they had been friends. And then, over the last couple of years, the friendship had grown into something more. Johannes thought about her even when he wasn't with her. And for about a year now, Sietske had been blushing every time they met.

Every summer they'd gone fishing or bicycling together whenever they had free time. But this year Sietske had been sent to an aunt's for three weeks. Her parents found it too risky for their daughter to meet with the son of a collaborator.

Johannes couldn't blame them. Who could be trusted in time of war? People who used to be friends had become enemies. His own family had lost friends because his father was a member of the wrong party. Mother's only sister, Aunt Alie, who lived in Harlingen, didn't want anything to do with them anymore. He regretted his harsh words to Sietske this afternoon. It wasn't her fault. Hitler was to blame.

Back home, Johannes helped his father put the shaft on the wheelbarrow. They didn't say much. He wasn't in the mood for talking.

"What's bothering you, Johannes?" Father finally asked as he wiped his greasy hands on a rag. "Is it me? I know how you feel about me being a member of the party and lately, I'm not sure . . . "

"Why don't you quit, Father? Everybody says the war will be over soon. What will they do with collaborators like you?" Johannes stood up and walked away. He didn't want to hear his father's answer. What could Father say? That lately he regretted being a member? Well, it was a little late for regrets. He should have thought of that more than four years ago.

Mother and Anneke worked in the vegetable garden, harvesting the last vegetables for the winter. He knew Anneke didn't like the work, but Mother kept her busy. Work seemed to be the only thing that kept his mother going these days. Her hair had turned grey in the last few years, and even though they had enough to eat, her face seemed much thinner. On the farm there was always plenty of food. But the war was wearing her down in other ways. He felt sorry for his sister. She had no one to play with. She'd always loved school, but for the last year she had been teased as well. Didn't his father realize what he was doing to them?

Later in the afternoon, the cows had to be milked again. At least he could forget about the war when he felt a cow's warm body against him. He concentrated on the milking, making sure every last drop was in the pail, so the animal wouldn't get an infection.

After supper Johannes checked the calves. One of them had seemed listless earlier. It stood by itself, away from the others. He couldn't really tell if it was sick. He went to the meadow where the sheep grazed, as he did every evening now. His father had asked him to count them. Lately, quite a few had gone missing. Father suspected that people from the village came down the canal in a boat during the night to steal the sheep. But it was hard to catch the thieves. Even though there was a curfew from eight in the evening until six in the morning, it was easy to steer a rowboat down the canal in the dark.

When he went inside, his mother was pulling down the blackout curtains. No light escaped through the windows. Some people used black paper, but Mother had sewn black curtains for every window in the house. The sides of the curtains had to be pinned to the wall with thumbtacks.

"Did you count the sheep?" she asked.

"Yes, the same as last night," Johannes answered. "Forty-one."

"Would you like something to drink? I canned some carrots today and there's some leftover juice."

The carbide lamp shone a white light on the table. Father's head bent over the newspaper. Bijke lay at his feet, his black and white paws crossed over his father's warm, woollen socks. Propaganda news from the party, Johannes guessed. Other newspapers were not allowed anymore.

"I hope the weather stays like this," Mother said. "The garden has never given us this much."

"Are you going to bed now, Johannes?" Father asked. "You'd better get some sleep before the sirens start. We haven't had much lately."

"Yes. Good night," he answered.

But instead of going straight to his room, Johannes tiptoed down the hall, grabbed his jacket and quietly opened the front door. He sneaked outside in his socks, leaving his shoes behind. There he waited. No sound. They hadn't heard him. He walked across the front lawn, climbed the fence and disappeared into the dark.

# Under the Bridge

Johannes hurried to the other end of the meadow. Following the canal to the bridge, he stayed low. There might be people hiding out there during curfew. Hawthorn bushes, which grew on the slope, scratched his arms and legs. He slid to the road on his stomach and ran across the bridge. He hid quickly behind some underbrush. In the distance he saw the lights of a car — it could only be German. Johannes crouched down and held his head close to the ground. What if they saw him? He didn't want to think about it. After the car passed, he crawled further.

The farm building of Sietske's family loomed in front of him like a black monster. Why had he come, anyway? Did he seriously think she would be here to meet him after what he'd said this afternoon? Ten o'clock and the field seemed strangely quiet. He watched the farm. Without the light of the moon, there wasn't much to see. He sat and waited for what felt like hours. Finally, he heard something rustle in the reeds along the canal. He held his breath.

"Johannes," whispered a voice.

"Sietske," he called softly. The outline of a shadow moved slowly in his direction in a crouched-down position. Carefully he crept towards her, until he heard her breathing.

He reached for her arms and pulled her down beside him in the grass. "You shouldn't have come. It's foolish. It's dangerous."

"I know," she sighed, and leaned her head against his shoulder.

He slipped his arm around her. They sat under the bridge and didn't speak until her breathing quieted.

"How did you get away?" he asked finally.

"Mother, Father and Klaas had a meeting with a member of the resistance. They had to talk about Bauke."

Johannes remained silent. He didn't want to interrupt. Sietske controlled how much she wanted to tell him, how much she trusted him. Gently he squeezed her shoulder.

"Bauke's in hiding," she continued. "I don't know why and I don't know where he is. Father said the less I know, the smaller the risk of endangering my brother. I wasn't allowed in the kitchen where they had the meeting. Klaas turned eighteen last month. He is now officially a member of the resistance, too. I told them I was tired and wanted to go to bed early. The visitor didn't leave until ten. Then I waited till my parents and Klaas went to bed before I could sneak out the door." A sigh escaped her lips.

Johannes took her hand in his.

Sietske spoke again. "I wanted to see you, but I didn't know if you would come after the things we said this afternoon. I do trust you, Johannes. It's just that sometimes it's very hard. My parents don't even want to hear your name."

"I behaved foolishly, Sietske. I was selfish. I didn't realize how difficult it must be for you. You have to listen to your parents. You can't blame them for not trusting anybody from my family. But I swear to you, Sietske, I do not share my father's beliefs. I wish he wasn't a member of the party. If he didn't want to be in the resistance, at least he could have stayed neutral. And I don't know why he isn't quitting now." Perspiration beaded his forehead.

"It's all right," Sietske spoke softly. "We can't let anything come between us. Not even our parents' beliefs."

"Are you sure?"

"Yes," she said.

He heard the determination in her voice and felt warm inside. "You are so brave," he whispered. Filled with pride, he smiled in the dark night.

Quietly, they sat with their own thoughts, the only sound the murmuring of the water in the canal.

"Do you still listen to the English radio at night?" he asked at last.

"Yes, every night at seven we listen to the BBC and Radio Orange. Do you?"

"No. My father turned our good radio over to the Germans to show he's a true party member. We secretly kept our old one. He has it hidden in the pantry and only listens to the German station. One night when my father was out, Mother and I tried to find the British station, but there was too much static."

"The Allied troops have moved through Belgium and are now at Arnhem, ready to cross the rivers and free us," she said. "Everyone says the war will be over soon. I can't wait."

Johannes nodded in agreement. How he wished it would end soon.

"Have you heard about the new organization, *NBS*, the Dutch Interior Armed Forces?"

Johannes shook his head. He chewed his bottom lip. How he hated that he never knew anything. He heard all the news from other people like Sietske, Douwe and the blacksmith.

"They are the new Dutch army. Prince Bernhard is the chief commander of these troops. Bauke says they will help the Allied armies liberate the rest of our country. Many young men who were in hiding have joined them."

"Good," Johannes answered. "The more there are, the sooner they'll be here to free us."

A bird called in the darkness of the evening.

"You have to go back, before the air raids begin," he said quietly.

"Not yet," she whispered. "Let's pretend there's no war. Just for a few more minutes."

"All right," he said and held her close. He listened for the sirens and felt the tension building inside him, but he couldn't let her go.

Suddenly she turned her head and kissed his lips. "I must go."

He helped her up. "When will I see you again, Sietske?" he whispered.

"I'll try Monday. Same time." She disappeared into the night. He stood and watched her dark shadow moving away from him.

Without any warning, the sirens screamed through the peaceful night. A moment later, he heard a yelp. It was Sietske.

In a few seconds he reached her and crouched beside her in the reeds. "What happened?"

"I stepped in a hole and twisted my ankle," she gasped.

"Oh God, Sietske. What do we do now?"

"I don't know," she said. "It's so dark out. The sirens startled me."

"I'll carry you home. I don't care if your father sees me."

"No! We can't risk it."

In the distance, they heard the familiar drone of the English bombers. Johannes picked Sietske up in his arms and carried her back under the bridge.

"Will they look for you?" she asked.

"Yes," Johannes answered. "If I don't go downstairs to the shelter my mother will come looking. What about you?"

"Same thing," she sighed. "We have a cellar in the barn. That's where we hide every night."

The sound of the planes grew closer. He held her tight. Her heart beat against his chest. What if a bomb hit the bridge? They sat holding each other for the next fifteen minutes. Light flashes soared across the sky. They heard the *ta-ta-ta* of the anti-aircraft guns, the high screaming of the Messerschmidts and the short staccato of the cannons. Spitfires seared over low, to scare off the German fighters. More planes criss-crossed the sky than on any other night.

The earth shook under the barrage of explosives. The concrete bridge shuddered. Bombs dropped from the sky like huge hailstones. Sietske trembled in Johannes' arms. He felt perspiration running down his forehead. They heard more planes, German fighters, trying to intercept the English bombers. A Messerschmidt roared low over the bridge. The sound echoed through their bones. Light flashes swept under and beside the bridge, attacking them with sharp, frightening shadows. They remained frozen in their embrace until the last plane had gone and the sirens had ceased. An eerie silence blanketed the earth.

Johannes wiped his forehead with the sleeve of his jacket. A chill night breeze made them shiver. Johannes' stocking feet felt frozen.

"I'll help you home. Or close to home," he added, when he felt her resistance.

"Who is there?" A voice boomed from the direction of the canal.

Sietske jumped. "It's me, Father. I'm okay." To Johannes she whispered, "Go."

He held on to her.

"Who is with you? I said, who is with you? Is it Johannes?" Sietske's father loomed before them.

"Yes, it's me, Mr. Dijkstra. Sietske has a sprained ankle," Johannes answered in a firm voice.

"I told you not to meet him again," he thundered.

"I asked her to meet me tonight," Johannes said.

"Go home, Johannes," Mr. Dijkstra said. "Your parents must be worried. If you ever come near my daughter again, I'll break both your legs!" He snatched his daughter from Johannes and carried her away.

For as long as he could see them, Johannes watched the two figures recede into the dark. Then slowly he turned and climbed up onto the bridge. The northeast sky was ablaze. The bombers had done their job. Had they finally flattened the air base? Or were civilians once again the main victims of this futile war?

# Minne

The worn green door opened before he could knock. His friend Minne stepped outside. They were the same height, but there the resemblance ended. Johannes had dark, straight hair, while Minne had curly, bright red hair. Johannes' face was tanned dark from the sun; Minne's skin was fair with freckles. He wore a grey jacket made of coarse wool, patched corduroy pants and wooden shoes. His normally sparkling blue eyes looked dull and distant.

"What's going on, Minne?" Johannes asked.

"We'd better not go inside. My mother's pretty upset these days. Let's go for a walk."

Johannes and Minne walked away from the house. "Has something happened to your father?" Johannes dug his hands deep into the pockets of his old blue jacket.

"Yes." Minne kicked at the cobblestones in the road. "The food the men get to eat in the German factories is worse than what we feed the pigs. The barracks they sleep in are cold and humid. My father's body can't take it. He is sick and too weak to travel home."

Johannes remained silent. He dug his fingernails into his skin. He didn't know what to say. Eight months ago, Minne's father had been sent to Germany to work in one of the weapons factories. The *Arbeitseinsatz* [slave labour] had taken many men from this area. They had been rounded up like cattle. For every German soldier at the front, they needed a replacement worker in their factories.

Minne and his mother had been devastated when he'd left. The conditions in the factories were inhumane. In addition, many factories had become targets for the Allied bombers.

"Can't you send him any good food?" Johannes finally asked.

"We did that many times, but my mother doubts he ever saw it."

"What if somebody got him out by car and drove him home?"

"Who has a car these days?" Minne barked. "You? How do you intend to cross the German border?"

"I don't know. I just wish I could do something." Johannes felt an anger he couldn't put into words.

They walked out of the village and took the gravel road past the church. They met no one.

After a long silence Minne spoke. "I'll do something about it. I'll take revenge. If my father dies, I'll kill every German soldier I can get my hands on." Minne raised his arms and showed his two fists. He stopped and turned to face Johannes. His voice rose. "I'm not kidding, Johannes. And I'll kill every collaborator I know." His eyes narrowed.

"You should come home with me then," Johannes taunted. "You can start by killing my father." He turned and began to walk away.

Minne dropped his arms and followed. "No," he said. "I could never kill your father, but I will join the resistance."

"They'll never let you in. You're too young. You have to be eighteen. And it's dangerous, Minne. The Germans are getting scared. They've become ruthless."

"The resistance isn't that strict about age anymore. If I tell them I'm eighteen, I think they'll believe me."

The sun warmed the two friends as they walked past the cemetery and the church. "I know you won't believe it," Johannes sighed, "but I wish I could sign up for the resistance, too."

"You! Come on, Johannes. Don't be a fool. You've no chance. They'd never let you." Minne's hand combed through his red curls.

"What if I used a different name?"

"They'd check you out first. It would be too dangerous if you joined. You could get information from both sides."

"I don't get information from my father!" Johannes' voice shook. "I don't know what he does! He never talks about it." He halted and rubbed his forehead. "What do you want me to do? Take sides?"

Minne stood face to face with Johannes. "If you did, who would you protect, Johannes? Your father? Or your friend Minne?"

"I would never turn my back on you, and you know that," Johannes bristled, then pushed past him.

Minne caught up with him. "Don't say that, Johannes. This is war! You have to make choices. You can't trust anybody. Not even your best friend. Our friendship is over. I'm joining. I've wasted too many years already. I can't stand by helplessly and watch my father die a slow, unnecessary death because of those bastards."

They turned around and walked back in silence. A sinking feeling came over Johannes. It slowly crept through his arms and legs. A tiredness filled his body.

An unfamiliar bicycle stood parked against the wall of Minne's house. "Wait outside for me," Minne said. "We

26

have a visitor." He opened the door and walked inside. The door closed behind him.

In the silence of the afternoon, Johannes could hear murmuring voices. A deep, male voice dominated the conversation. Johannes waited. He felt empty, knowing he had lost something — something important. He stirred as the door opened again. Minne, his face an ashen white, walked towards him.

"Is he . . . is it your father?" Johannes fumbled.

Minne stood in front of him. A mixture of anger and hate filled his white face. His eyes narrowed.

"Not yet," he whispered. "He's in a hospital in Germany. But it's too late. The infection has spread to his lungs. The hospital has no medication to treat infections." Minne grabbed Johannes' shoulders. "He's going to die, Johannes. He's going to die." He began to tremble. Johannes grabbed his arms.

The hate left Minne's blue eyes. Pain filled them before he collapsed onto Johannes' shoulder, his body shaking with sobs. Johannes held his friend. He felt nothing but an emptiness he couldn't describe and an aching pain in his stomach.

Minne let go. He stepped away. "Go home, Johannes." His voice sounded hollow. He dried his face on the sleeve of his jacket, then let his arms hang limply beside his body.

Johannes wished he knew what to say. He wished he could do something to reverse the fate of this kind man, his friend's father. "Is there anything you need? Can I do something for your mother?"

"No. We can manage. You'd better go. It's no use hanging around. I'm going in to look after my mother." He turned and walked inside, gently closing the door.

On the way home, Johannes couldn't shake the feeling that Minne had meant it when he'd said their friendship was over. Had he now lost both his friends?

Minne and Sietske? Perhaps he hadn't lost Sietske, but after her father had found them under the bridge the night of the violent air raid, the chances of seeing her again were slim.

That night the air base had been completely destroyed at a cost of seven civilian lives. His parents had been waiting up for him. His father had looked puzzled, but he hadn't said a word. Mother had been upset. He could still see the pain in her face. He didn't want to hurt his mother. It wasn't her fault. But as for his father, he wanted to hurt the man, just as he'd been hurt, like his sister had been hurt.

When Johannes returned home, Father and Douwe were rounding up the cows. He'd lost track of time while spending the afternoon with Minne.

"You're late, Johannes! Where were you?" Father's normally calm voice sounded impatient.

Johannes didn't answer.

His father grabbed his sleeve. "I asked you a question and I expect an answer."

A feeling of disgust came over Johannes, engulfing him. "I hate you!" he cried. "Can't you see what you are doing to us? We've lost our friends. We are despised by the community. I hate you!" He turned and briskly walked back towards the house.

"Wait!" His father followed him. "What happened this afternoon, Johannes?"

Johannes stopped. Slowly he turned around. "Minne's father is dying because your friends in Germany have treated him like . . . worse than an animal." Then he ran all the way to the house.

In his room Johannes threw himself on the bed. He remembered all the things he and Minne had learned from Minne's father. And in the privacy of his own space he finally let go, releasing the emotions that he had tried so hard to hold inside.

# Visitors

"A cow! A whole cow!" His mother's voice sounded high and shrill.

Johannes waited before opening the door into the kitchen.

"Yes, they need meat for the troops and they have ordered me to give a cow," his father's voice answered calmly.

Johannes felt uneasy. His mother never yelled.

"There are so many of our own people who need food. In Amsterdam small children and old people are dying of starvation. I will not give food to the German soldiers!"

"They'll be here tomorrow morning at six. I suggest you don't try to stop them."

Bang. The inside door slammed. His mother had left the kitchen to go to their bedroom.

Slowly Johannes released his breath, but the tension remained in his body. Anger surged through him as he opened the kitchen door and raged, "Which one are you going to offer your friends?"

His father was standing in front of the window, his back to the room. At Johannes' outburst, he swung around. His face had turned a greyish colour. Deep shadows marked his eyes. "I think Afke would be best. She doesn't have a wealth of meat, but I don't want to lose . . . "

"You think they want something a little more lean for their elite troops at the front," Johannes sneered.

"I don't have a choice, Johannes. At least we have to send only one cow. Other farmers have to give up five." His voice sounded tired.

Johannes sat down at the table. "We are so lucky that you are a member of the party. We only have to give up *one* cow!" His fist hit the table.

"Johannes! Don't speak to me like that! And don't interfere in this matter! You and I will never agree!"

"Why don't you resign from the party, Father? Why?"

Father sighed and gazed out the window. In a soft voice he said, "Tell your mother I'll be back before milking time," then left the kitchen.

Johannes stared out the window and rested his head on his hands. Rain slapped against the glass pane. Fallen leaves from the two lindens covered the front yard. One more October storm and the trees would be bare. The outside coldness crept into Johannes' heart.

Rumours that the war would be over had soon diminished. Earlier in the fall, the southern part of the Netherlands had been freed by Allied troops. But by late October, the Allies still hadn't crossed the rivers Rhine and Maas. The Germans, who had sustained heavy losses on the eastern fronts, dug themselves in at the two rivers.

Now that the animals stayed inside due to the cold, wet weather, there wasn't much work to do. After feeding and milking, Johannes' time spent in the barn consisted mostly of chores like cleaning out the manure, forking hay in the loft and changing the straw underneath the cows once a day. During this slack time, he and Douwe cut trees for firewood. Much to the dismay of his wife, Douwe didn't hide under the counter in the cabinets anymore.

These days Johannes had a lot of time to think. He'd lost all contact with Minne. Every time he went into the village and tried to visit, Minne's mother said he wasn't home. Minne's father had died and his body had been buried in hostile soil. No doubt Minne had joined the resistance and was probably actively involved in sabotaging the Germans. A sigh escaped Johannes' lips as he looked out the window. Oh, how he wished he could join, too.

Many nights he had waited under the bridge, but Sietske never showed up. Was it because she hadn't had a chance to meet him, or because she'd chosen not to? All he'd heard of Sietske was that she didn't attend school anymore. Her parents thought it too dangerous for her to bike the ten kilometres into town. These days, the Allied bombings occurred in the daylight as well as at night. Their targets were mainly trains, in an attempt to prevent cargo from reaching Germany and to slow down the movement of troops. German soldiers also took bicycles from people. Even children's bikes were not safe anymore. It seemed that stealing had become one of their main occupations.

Just then a black car turned into the long driveway of the van der Meer farm. Germans. Johannes moved away from the glass. He didn't want to be seen by his father's friends. The car drove around to the barn. He went upstairs to his room. From his window he could see the roof of Sietske's farm and he had a good view of the bridge.

Later, as the car left the farm, Johannes could just make out his father's cap through the rear window. The car turned right, in the direction of Leeuwarden. Johannes slouched on the seat at the window sill. The sky, grey and dull, seemed threatening today. His eyes followed the direction of the canal. Nothing moved except for the reeds along the water.

Something on the bridge caught Johannes' eye. He squinted to see better. It appeared to be a woman pushing a baby carriage. She seemed to be an older person, wearing a long black coat and a scarf around her head. Her back bent, she pushed the carriage across the road into their driveway. Suddenly, she started running towards the farm.

Johannes jumped up and ran downstairs. His mother was probably too upset to answer the door. It must be a woman from one of the big cities where food had become scarce. His mother always gave those people milk and butter. He would help the woman and her baby. But when he opened the front door, Johannes didn't see her or the carriage. He stepped outside in the rain to see if she had gone around to the back door. It was raining heavily now, so he grabbed his coat and boots before heading out.

It was strange that the woman hadn't knocked at the front door, Johannes thought. He went around to the laundry room and the stable. Then the tracks of the baby carriage caught his eye. They led to the barn where the tractor and other farm equipment were stored. The shed stood about fifty metres from the main farm building.

Taking giant steps to avoid the puddles, Johannes ran to the building. The door stood ajar and he could hear the crying of a baby. Not wanting to startle the woman, he coughed before he entered the barn. The woman stood with her back to him. She held the baby in her arms and rocked it gently. There was something familiar about the woman.

"Excuse me," Johannes started. "You should have come to the front door. It is too cold for your baby in this barn."

Slowly, the woman turned around to face him. "I couldn't go to your front door, Johannes."

"Sietske!" He stumbled to get to her. "You are soaked. Whose baby are you holding? Why are you here?"

Her lips, blue from the cold, trembled. The baby had stopped crying and was sucking fervently on the fringes of the blanket wrapped around her.

"There was a roundup of people hiding at the farm." Tears ran down her face.

Johannes threw his arms around her and the baby. "Oh my God, Sietske. How did you get away?"

"We were tipped off. Someone came to the farm and told us to make sure all the people in hiding were gone. Mother told me to take the baby and leave. She said she'd look after the parents. I'm so scared, Johannes. If the Germans find Natalie's parents, they will kill them all — my parents and brothers included."

She trembled in his arms. Johannes felt helpless. What could he do for her? One look at the little dark-haired baby told him she was probably Jewish. How could anybody hate a little baby?

"You can't stay here, Sietske. Come inside with me. My father is gone. He won't be back until later this afternoon. You can trust my mother."

She nodded and slowly followed him into the house. The living quarters were quiet. Anneke was at school and wouldn't be home until four. Douwe's wife, who helped his mother in the mornings, had gone home.

Johannes pulled up a chair in front of the wood-stove. He helped Sietske take off her wet coat and coaxed her and the baby into the chair. With his calloused hand, he wiped a tear from her cheek, then went in search of his mother.

The bedroom door was closed. He knocked. "Mother," he called.

"Yes," a tired voice answered.

"Will you help me, Mother? Sietske is here with a Jewish baby. There's a roundup at their farm."

"Oh my God!" He heard his mother jump out of bed and cross the room. "I'll be right there."

Johannes returned to the kitchen. Sietske was rocking the baby, who'd started to cry again. He walked over to the window.

"Where's your father?" Sietske's voice sounded harsh.

"He went in the direction of town." Johannes felt a knot in his stomach. What if his father had something to do with the roundup? No! No! "He wouldn't do anything like this to his neighbours, Sietske."

"Are you sure?" she asked.

Johannes didn't answer. He wasn't sure of anything anymore. But if his father *was* involved in the rounding up of people, he would . . .

The door to the kitchen opened. His mother entered, her hair combed away from her face, her eyes full of concern. She stared at Sietske and the baby.

"You can't stay here, Sietske," she said in a calm voice. "The Nazis will drive my husband home in a couple of hours, and although they never come into the living quarters, we can't risk it. First you both need something to eat. Does the baby drink diluted milk?"

"Yes," Sietske answered. "We often feed her that, too, if her mother doesn't have enough. Mother sent me away because the baby cries a lot. I didn't know where to go." Helplessly, she looked from Johannes to his mother. "Thank you, Mrs. van der Meer," she added.

Johannes' mother busied herself with milk she'd poured into a small pan on the stove. "I'll make you some too, Sietske," she said. Johannes noticed a softness in his mother's eyes when she looked at the baby.

The baby had to be fed without a bottle. Sietske and his mother tried to pour the milk into the infant's mouth with a cup and a small spoon. She made quite a mess, but they managed to give her some. Not many words were spoken in the farm kitchen. They all had their own thoughts.

"Can't we hide her until it's dark?" Johannes suggested.

"I would like to," his mother answered. "Perhaps we can keep your father out of the house. If he is still mad at me, he might go straight to the stable and milk the cows when he returns. Let me think about this, Sietske. For now you're safe."

"Do you think they'll take my parents?" Sietske asked in a trembling voice.

"I don't know, Sietske," his mother answered. "Let's hope they don't find the people you're hiding."

Sietske nodded. She stared at the woodstove. The baby had fallen asleep in her arms. Johannes watched her for a few seconds, keeping one eye on the road. Her face was pale and blue circles framed her brown eyes. Their sparkle had gone. He felt an overwhelming urge to protect her.

"There!" He pointed to the road. Two military trucks passed by, moving in the direction of the village. "I'm sure they came from your place, Sietske."

She turned to him. Anxiety tightened the muscles of her face. "I have to go home," she said. "I must find out what has happened to everybody."

Then a black car turned into the van der Meer driveway.

"Oh no! It's Father! With the Germans!" Johannes grabbed Sietske and pushed her and the baby in the direction of the bedrooms. "Quick! Mother, we have to hide them!"

His mother's face showed no emotion. "Johannes, go to the stable. Get the milking equipment organized for the afternoon milking and make sure he doesn't come inside. Come with me, Sietske." She opened the door to the bedrooms.

Johannes didn't wait. He went through the kitchen and the laundry room to the far end of the stable, where the milk pails were kept on a rack. He heard the engine of the car outside the stable door. A door slammed. His heart beat in his throat. In his distress Johannes dropped two pails. The sound of metal upon metal filled his ears. When the door of the stable opened, he tensed.

His father walked in. Alone.

# Safe?

"You're early, Johannes," his father said when he saw Johannes gathering the milk pails.

"I didn't know if you would be back in time," he answered.

"Where's your mother?"

"In the kitchen." Johannes busied himself with the pails so he didn't have to look at his father's face.

"Your face tells me I'd better not go inside." He walked to the laundry room where he kept a change of milking clothes.

Johannes sighed with relief. "I'll go up and throw down the hay!" he called. Up in the hayloft, he raked portions of hay together and pushed them through the openings. The hay landed in front of the cows. For every two cows there was an opening in the floor of the hayloft. Immediately after finishing his chores he would help Sietske home.

Sietske. The baby carriage! He had to hide it! It still stood in the storage shed for everyone to see. As soon as he finished feeding the cows, Johannes climbed down the ladder. He didn't see his father. Quickly he opened the barn door and ran out in the rain to the shed. The door stood half open. He pushed it further with his arm and stepped inside.

The carriage was gone.

Catching his breath, Johannes wondered if his mother had taken the carriage. Or maybe Sietske. That meant Sietske was gone. His father must not know that he was here. He didn't want any questions. He checked around once more. Then he closed the door and ran back to the stable.

The door opened and there stood his father. "What were you up to, Johannes?" he asked. "I saw you running to the shed as if someone was chasing you."

Johannes felt colour burn his cheeks. "I had to check on something." His father's eyebrows rose. "I'd better get to work," Johannes added.

He walked into the stable to get his milking pail and found his first cow. For a moment he rested his wet head against its warm body. His heartbeat slowly returned to normal. Why couldn't he just say to his father that Sietske was hiding in their house with a Jewish baby? He hated to sneak around like this. What would happen if he did confront his father? No, he couldn't risk it. Too many lives were at stake. Swearing softly, he rubbed the udder of the cow.

Douwe arrived and started milking, sitting himself two cows ahead of Johannes. His father sat at the far end of the stable. The familiar sounds of cows chewing, tails swishing and milk spraying against the metal of the pails didn't soothe Johannes. His thoughts ran around in circles again. Had his father known about the raid at Sietske's farm? Did he have anything to do with the rounding up of people in hiding? Had he been there this afternoon?

"I think that cow is long finished! Johannes?" His

father's voice startled him. Johannes jumped off his stool and almost knocked over the pail. He had better keep his wits about him. How else could he help Sietske?

After milking, he fed the calves.

"Johannes," his mother called, "can you bring me some milk as soon as you're done?"

"Yes, Mother." He hurried to carry the pails to Douwe to be cleaned. Then he rushed to get the milk pan from his mother.

"When you come inside with the milk," she said softly, "take your boots and your rain slicker with you. Sietske is waiting for you at the front door." She handed the pan to Johannes.

He almost ran to the other end of the stable where the milk was kept in cans. The next morning it would be picked up by horse and wagon to be taken to the milk factory in the village. Most of the milk was seized by the Germans, but his family kept some milk to trade with people who came to the farm during the day.

He had to walk back carefully so he didn't spill the milk. His mother opened the door to the kitchen. The sound of footsteps came up suddenly behind him. His father.

"How soon can you have the evening meal ready?" he asked. "I have to go out after."

"It will be ready in ten minutes," she said calmly.

His father nodded and turned and walked towards the far end of the barn. Taking the milk pan from Johannes, his mother said, "Hurry. Move as fast as you can. You don't want to meet a German car in the driveway."

Johannes grabbed his slicker from the hook and took his boots. He dashed to the kitchen . . . then stopped in his tracks. At the kitchen table sat Anneke, shaking a glass bottle filled with cream to make butter. He'd forgotten all about her.

Anneke saw his shocked face. She smiled. "Don't worry, Johannes. I can keep a secret."

"Thanks," he said, and tugged one of her long, blond braids.

In the hallway stood Sietske, with the baby in the carriage. She wore the now dried coat with the scarf around her head. She opened the door and together they lifted the carriage down the two concrete steps outside.

His mother followed them to the doorway. "Hurry, Johannes. Be back before curfew."

"Thank you for helping, Mrs. van der Meer," Sietske said.

Mother closed the front door behind them. The rain still fell in the darkened evening. Without a word, Sietske and Johannes pushed the carriage over the uneven path. The baby started to whimper.

"What will we do if there are cars on the road?" Sietske asked.

"We'll push the carriage into the bushes along the road. We have to try and hide, too. Let's hurry. My father will be picked up by the Germans again. We mustn't let them see us."

They hurried down the driveway. They could see no lights from either direction as they crossed the road.

"Keep your eyes on the road ahead. I'll look behind us," Johannes panted.

Sietske didn't answer. Just before they reached the bridge, she called, "A car! Quick! Take cover!"

Together they bounced the carriage into the hawthorn bushes until it was out of sight. The baby's crying grew louder. They crouched down close to the ground. The rain had made the area slippery. Holding on to the carriage, Johannes steadied Sietske while they moved down the slope beside the bridge. Her breath came in short gulps.

"Are you all right?" he asked quietly.

A military truck passed by. They didn't move.

"I'm afraid to go home," she said. "Perhaps my parents have been picked up. Natalie's father and mother could be dead."

"Stop it!" he ordered. "Once we're close to your farm, you hide with the baby behind the house. I'll go in first."

"But, Johannes, I don't want you to — "

"Yes, I will," he said firmly. "I can't join the resistance. This is the only thing I can do for you. Please let me, Sietske."

"All right," she sighed. "I'll get up to see if it's safe to go now. You hang on to the carriage." She pulled herself up and crawled to the road. "Let's go," she said.

"Take the baby," Johannes said. "We can get the carriage later."

Sietske draped the little infant in a blanket and held it in her arms, close to her body. Johannes pushed the carriage down into the bushes.

Quickly they climbed up the slope. Mud stuck to their shoes. As fast as they could, they walked over the bridge. Without further interruptions they made it to the long driveway of her farm.

To one side of the living quarters towered two ancient chestnut trees. They slipped behind the trees, then ran for the side of the stable.

"You and the baby hide behind the stable," Johannes said. "I'll find out what happened this afternoon. When everything is safe, I'll come and get you."

Natalie, who had stopped crying, now began to whimper. Johannes rearranged the blanket around the tiny body. Unbuttoning her coat, Sietske tucked the infant inside. Johannes wrapped his arms around Sietske and bent his head. She leaned her forehead against his. They stood motionless. The rain dripped from their hair.

"Go," he whispered as his lips touched hers. Gently, he pushed her around the corner of the stable. He waited until she disappeared. Then he followed the path to the front door. Instead of knocking, he walked along the front of the house to the kitchen window. He put his ear near the glass pane. He could hear several voices, none of them recognizable.

It was risky, but he couldn't leave Sietske out in the rain with the baby. He knocked on the window. The voices stopped. Wodan, the black farm dog, growled. He heard footsteps. A few moments later, the front door opened.

"Who is it?" a woman's voice said.

"It's me, Johannes, Mrs. Dijkstra."

"Come in. I hoped it was Sietske," the woman answered. Johannes heard the quiver in her voice.

"Are you all right? Is everybody else here? I mean, is it safe for Sietske to come home?" He kept his voice down, afraid there were ears that shouldn't hear him.

"No, it's not all right, Johannes," Sietske's mother said. "Sietske and the baby can come in, though. The Nazis have gone, but they've taken my husband."

Johannes stared at Mrs. Dijkstra in disbelief. "Is . . . is everybody else safe?" He stumbled through the question.

"Yes," Sietske's mother answered. "They didn't find anybody. But they were convinced we were hiding Jewish people. They took my husband to try to make me admit it. Where is Sietske?"

"Close by. I'll go and get her," he said.

Johannes ran to the stable where he found Sietske leaning against the wall under the overhanging roof. His arms went around her and he pulled her to him, being careful not to crush the baby.

"You can tell me, Johannes. I know something is wrong," she said before Johannes could speak.

"It's your father, Sietske. They took him out of revenge because they didn't find anybody. They were sure you had people in hiding."

"Oh, no." A sob escaped her throat. She started to tremble.

"You people are so brave," Johannes said. "You risk your own lives to save strangers."

Sietske sighed. "At this moment I wish we hadn't. I wish we'd never taken these people in. My father might have to pay for this with his life."

"Shh, don't say that, Sietske. If there isn't any evidence, they'll release him." He didn't know why he said that. Did he believe the Germans would be that fair? Lately, they had murdered the people who were hiding others, to set an example and to scare anyone else who might be brave enough to do the same.

"Go inside," he said. With his arm around her waist, he walked her to the front door. "I'd better leave now," he added. "I'm sure your mother doesn't need to see me again."

"No," she said resolutely. "I want you to come inside with me. I want you to stay for a while."

He nodded. "I'll stay."

They pushed the door open and walked into the hall, where they left their wet clothing. A soft light shone from under the kitchen door. With the baby in her arms, Sietske opened the door. Johannes followed behind her. Several people sat rigidly around the kitchen table. Sietske's mother rose from her chair, as did a young woman whom he'd never seen before. Johannes took in the others at the table — Klaas, Bauke, next to him a young man with short black hair and dark, piercing eyes.

Beside the young man, at the end of the table, sat Minne.

# The Confrontation

"Minne!" He didn't know what else to say.

"Surprised?"

Johannes nodded.

"Sit down." Mrs. Dijkstra pulled out a chair for him.

Sietske helped the young woman, who he knew must be Natalie's mother, change the baby. The young father and the other three men in the room never took their eyes off him. He felt tension — or hostility — in the air, as if it were his fault all this had happened.

He cleared his throat. "I'm very sorry they took your husband, Mrs. Dijkstra."

She didn't answer but poured everybody a cup of substitute coffee, made with milk and chicory. Sietske and her mother were very much alike. They both had the same eyes, the same build and the same brown, curly hair, except Mrs. Dijkstra's was streaked with grey.

"Johannes and his mother kept me safe all afternoon," Sietske spoke up, as if she felt the tension, too. "His mother helped me get the carriage out of the shack, and Natalie and I stayed upstairs during milking time."

"Where was your father, Johannes?" Minne asked, his tone sharp. "If he found out about Sietske and the baby, nobody would be safe right now."

"My father wasn't home when Sietske arrived," Johannes replied. "And he was still working in the stable when we left. My mother kept him occupied until we had gone." He looked around the table. Everyone watched him as if he were on trial. All except for Sietske. For a split second their eyes met and held. That exchange gave him the courage to ask the question that had been on his mind all afternoon.

"Mrs. Dijkstra?" He waited. "Was . . . was my father one of them this afternoon?"

Her expression softened just for a second. "No. He wasn't with them."

A sigh escaped his lips. All eyes were upon him. He knew what they must be thinking. He looked at Bauke, Sietske's oldest brother. As if reading his thoughts, Bauke stood up from the table. Sietske rose as well.

"No, Sietske," Bauke said. "I want to talk to your friend alone. Come outside with me, Johannes."

Without a word Johannes followed Bauke into the hallway. Bauke, at twenty-two, was the same height as Johannes, but his build was heavier and more muscular. His eyes were the same as Sietske's, as was his brown, curly hair. Johannes admired Bauke. He wasn't a talker, but he'd always treated Johannes like a friend.

"Are you serious about my sister, Johannes?" Bauke asked as he opened the front door.

"Yes," Johannes answered.

"I thought so," Bauke said. They walked to the barn. It had stopped raining. "You are not interested in joining the party?"

Johannes stopped. "No." He looked at Bauke's face. "I don't agree with my father. I wish he were like your father."

"They might be torturing my father at this moment." Bauke dug his fists deep into his pockets. "He might even be dead."

Johannes had no answer to that. They continued walking. "What about Minne?" he ventured. "Why is he here?"

"You and Minne are best friends?"

"Not anymore. Not since his father died a few weeks ago. He wanted to join the resistance and said I could never be part of it." Johannes licked his dry lips. They stopped at a fence. The clouds were breaking up and the moon was making an attempt to slip through the gaps.

"It can't be easy for you." Bauke broke the silence. "You and your father on opposite sides."

"No, it isn't. I would like to join, too, Bauke. I would never betray any of you. I swear to that!" His voice had risen. His heart beat faster as he looked at the man beside him.

Bauke's expression was blank. He stared into the distance. It seemed he had forgotten Johannes' existence. "We'd better go back to the others."

Without another word they tramped back along the mud road to the living quarters. Before Bauke opened the door, he said in a low voice, "Sietske is my courier. She'll give you your assignments. But not a word to anybody in there."

Johannes nodded. He couldn't believe it. He grabbed Bauke's sleeve. "Thank you," he whispered.

Bauke shook his hand free. "Not one word, understand."

Then they heard it.

Bauke pulled Johannes with him to the side of the house. "There's someone here," he whispered. They stayed close to the wall. "Don't move. Listen. It sounds like there's someone coming down the path. When he comes around the corner, we'll jump him."

Johannes kept his eyes on the driveway. He heard the footsteps come nearer. They moved slowly. It sounded like a person limping instead of walking. That meant it wasn't a German soldier. They never came alone anyway. The moon lit the path.

As the person appeared, Bauke jumped ahead of him. Then he stopped in his tracks. "Father!" he gasped. "Where did you come from? What did they do to you?"

"Bauke, is that you?" The man reached for his son's arms. His breath came out in gulps. "I'm all right. Who is with you?"

"It's me, Johannes." Johannes stepped forward.

His neighbour frowned at him and shook his head. "You can't stay away from her, can you?"

"No, I can't, Mr. Dijkstra. And I won't." Johannes' heart beat hard against his rib cage.

"Why are you limping, Father?" Bauke interrupted.

"They thought they could scare me," he snorted. "I was taken to the House of Detention in Leeuwarden. The head of the security police was convinced we had people in hiding. Your mother didn't blink when they took me away." He swallowed. Johannes saw beads of perspiration trickle down the man's forehead. He'd taken off his cap.

"Questioning me didn't give them enough satisfaction, so they sent in some animal who had a good time with me." Mr. Dijkstra spit on the ground. Bauke held on to his father. "My eye will be purple for a couple of days, and my ankle is swollen. It will all be better soon. Johannes, I guess I have your father to thank for getting me out of further trouble."

Johannes' heart beat in this throat. "My father was there with the head of the security police? What did he do?"

"He didn't do anything. He is an interpreter. I didn't know he spoke German so well."

"Yes, he took German in school and he went to Germany a couple of times before the war," Johannes said. He couldn't believe his father helped the Germans that way.

"Anyway," Mr. Dijkstra continued, "I could make out most of what your father said. He told them that he'd never seen anybody at our place and that he would know because he was my neighbour and always kept an eye on me. Then they let me go. But I had to walk the twelve kilometres home. Every time I saw a car coming, I dove into a ditch, because I had no papers on me. Finally a man in a wagon gave me a ride. That's how I made it home before curfew."

Johannes exhaled long and deeply. He hadn't realized he'd been holding his breath.

"What your father does is not all bad. Maybe he saves more people. People like me . . . I don't know. But I sure don't like it when he comes with his friends to seize cattle for the German troops." Mr. Dijkstra spat on the ground in front of Johannes. "We better go inside so I can prove that they can't break me that easily." Mr. Dijkstra's bitter laugh echoed in Johannes' head.

When the three men stepped inside, a murmur of relief rippled around the kitchen. Mrs. Dijkstra, normally so talkative, suddenly became very busy at the stove, preparing food for her husband. Bauke and Klaas helped their father into a chair. Sietske pulled off his socks, which were stained with blood. She gently cleaned his ankle with warm water. The Jewish family had disappeared into their hiding place for the evening.

Minne still sat in the same spot without saying a word. Johannes wondered what business he had at the Dijkstras' farm.

Mrs. Dijkstra handed her husband a cup of coffee and a sandwich. "You'd better stay off your foot for a few days," she said.

"No, there's too much work to do!" he answered, his mouth full.

"We'll do the work, Father," Sietske said. "Minne is our new farm hand. He needs to work for food. His mother isn't well."

Mr. Dijkstra looked at Minne. "You will start tomorrow morning as soon as you can get here after curfew. Do you have a good bike?"

"Yes, Mr. Dijkstra." Minne rose. "I'll be here. I'd better go now before Mother starts to worry."

"Don't forget the package of bread, cheese and butter I wrapped for your mother." Mrs. Dijkstra bustled around.

"Thanks for everything." Minne stuck the package inside his shabby winter coat. He drew a brown knitted cap from his pocket and covered his head. He nodded at Mr. and Mrs. Dijkstra, opened the door and left.

"Wait!" Johannes followed his friend outside. "Minne, I'm sorry about your father. I heard he died at the end of September."

Minne stopped. He nodded, turned away and disappeared into the night.

Johannes' shoulders slumped. He returned to the kitchen. "I'd better go home, too," he announced. He looked at Sietske. She nodded and followed him outside.

"I'll walk you to the main road," she said, and grabbed his hand. "What did Bauke tell you tonight?"

"He said you are the courier. You will give me information, but I'm not to tell anybody." They stopped. Johannes turned and faced Sietske. "How dangerous is your work?"

She looked up into his eyes. "Oh, not very dangerous."

He stared back. "I don't believe you."

A warm smile lit up her face. She gently pinched his cheek. "You don't have to worry about me. I will be seventeen in the spring and I am perfectly capable of looking out for myself."

Johannes couldn't resist the gleam in her eyes. Arms wound around each other, they followed the path to the road.

"From now on I'll come to your place, Johannes.

We don't want your father to grow suspicious when you come here too often. Will your parents object if I come to see you?" Sietske laughed.

"No, I don't think so." Johannes smiled. He hadn't felt this good in a long time. At the main road he kissed Sietske long and hard, lifting her off the ground and twirling her around.

"Hey, what's gotten into you?" Sietske teased.

"Bring me some messages soon, my dear maiden. Don't make me wait too long, or I shall die."

"I will ride to your castle on my rusty old bike as often as I can, dear Prince Johannes. And now I must go. Curfew starts in a few minutes."

Johannes ran all the way home. He felt light with energy. As he opened the front door, he remembered Sietske's father's words, "I have your father to thank . . . " A bitter taste came into his mouth. He swallowed and hung up his coat. When he entered the kitchen and faced his father, the lightness left him.

"Where have you been, Johannes?" His father sat in his chair at the kitchen table. Mother sat on the opposite side, knitting a pair of socks out of handspun sheep's wool. Anneke looked up from her book.

"I went to see Sietske, Father," he answered, meeting his father's eyes.

"What are you up to, Johannes?" His voice cut the silence.

"I'm going out with Sietske. I hope that's all right with you." Johannes felt his whole body grow rigid.

"Did you see Sietske's father?" His voice quavered. "Did he get home?"

Mother looked at Johannes, her eyes full of questions. He nodded at her. "Yes," he answered. He felt like spitting at his father.

"Are you turning against your own father, Johannes?" His chair scraped across the wooden floor. In two strides he was standing in front of Johannes. Johannes still had to look up at him. He didn't flinch. His father's breathing came more quickly. His hands grabbed Johannes' shoulders. "Answer me!" he cried, shaking him.

Anneke gasped. Mother rose from her chair.

"Stop! That's enough, Durk! Let go of Johannes," she added in a firm voice.

Slowly his father's arms loosened their grip. He turned around and stumbled back to his chair. He sat down, took his glasses off and covered his face with his hands.

"Anneke and Johannes, go upstairs," Mother said. "We will talk about this tomorrow." Anneke looked from her father and mother to Johannes. Without a word, brother and sister trudged upstairs.

For a long time Johannes stared into the blackness of his room. Never before had he seen his father lose control. It was a while before sleep took away those haunting words *Are you turning against your own father, Johannes?*

# Butter for Aunt Siet

"Will you come to Franeker with me tomorrow afternoon? I have to take some butter to my aunt." Sietske leaned on her bike.

Through the small window in the stable, Johannes had seen her coming as he was getting the milk cans ready for transportation. He'd run outside to meet her. It was better to talk outside.

The wind, roaring in from the northeast, made it bitterly cold. Sietske wore a strange black coat. She saw the look on his face and laughed.

"I've outgrown all my clothes. This creation was designed by my mother, made from an old blanket and sewn by my mother and myself." She twirled around on her wooden shoes to show him front and back, and made a curtsy.

"An old blanket?"

"Yes." Her brown eyes sparkled. "There's a place in town where you can have fabric dyed."

"Does the colour run? What happens when it rains?"

"I didn't know you were interested in fashion, Johannes." She grabbed his arms. "No, it does not rub off, but it does fade very quickly. And if this damn war lasts much longer, I will be walking around in a pale pink blanket coat."

Johannes laughed. He admired her. She seemed to have an answer for everything. "I didn't know you had an aunt in Franeker," he said.

"You never ask a courier any questions," she answered, as she winked at him.

He raised his arm and tipped his cap. "What time do we leave? Or can't I ask that question either?" he teased.

"No," Sietske answered. "If you had given me a chance, I would have told you all you need to know. We leave at one in the afternoon and will be back at four in time for milking. Yes, you can tell your parents you are biking to Franeker with me to bring my aunt some butter. And now I must go." She put both arms around his neck and kissed him.

Before Johannes could take it all in, she was gone. The wind rose and he saw her push hard on her old bike. He whistled as he went back to his chores.

The next day the weather seemed worse. Wet snow mingled with rain, and a heavy northwestern storm met the two lonely bicyclists on their way to Franeker.

"Do you have the butter?" Johannes asked.

"Yes, all wrapped up and disguised in my saddlebags," she said.

"It's going to be hard to bike on that old thing of yours." He examined Sietske's vehicle. She had outgrown the bicycle by at least two sizes. The rubber on the tires had worn off and it squeaked like an old steam engine.

"Don't you dare insult my bike," she snapped. "Just think how fast we will sail on the way back when the wind is behind us."

Johannes laughed. Sietske grinned.

But the teenagers became serious when they met two older people on foot, pulling a homemade wagon. Their clothes were mere rags, their eyes hollow from lack of food.

"They must have been walking for days," Sietske said.

"Yes, there is no food left in the big cities. I heard people are dying of starvation. We're lucky we live on a farm."

They met more people on the road. Some carried crying children. Johannes felt a tightness growing in his chest. He saw how Sietske's eyes followed a family with five children. They wore ill-fitting clothing and looked more like moving skeletons than people.

Sometimes they had to bike behind each other to make room for wagons and baby carriages. It took them nearly an hour to cover the ten-kilometre distance to Franeker. As the water tower came into sight, so did a German truck. It was parked next to the road. Two German soldiers in shiny, black uniforms, with rifles over their shoulders, stood beside the cab. A man who had been pedalling ahead of them was stopped. They saw him take something out of his pocket and hand it to one of the soldiers. The German studied the paper, gave it back to the man and motioned for him to move along.

"Do you think they'll stop us?" Sietske said.

Johannes nodded.

"*Halt!*" The tallest of the two soldiers stepped in front of them.

Johannes and Sietske stopped their bicycles.

"*Ausweis, bitte* [Identity card, please]!" he said.

"*Wir haben keinen Ausweis* [We have no identity cards]," Johannes answered.

"*Wie alt bist du* [How old are you]?" the soldier asked.

"*Sechzehn* [sixteen]," Johannes answered.

Both Germans scanned him from top to bottom as if they needed some physical proof. "*Und du* [And you]?"

One of them pointed to Sietske.

"*Sechzehn,*" she answered.

"*Und was hast du da drin* [And what do you have in here]?" he said, as he pointed to the saddlebags.

"*Nichts* [Nothing]." Sietske shook her head.

"*Aufmachen* [Open up]!" he growled.

Johannes watched Sietske slowly unbuckle the saddlebags.

"*Schnell* [Quickly]!" The German stepped closer.

Sietske's eyes shot fire.

"Give it to him, Sietske," Johannes said quickly.

Sietske took out the parcel and handed it to the soldier. Interested, the other soldier stepped closer. "*Ein Geschenk für uns* [A gift for us]," he laughed. The first one unwrapped the tea towel. Then he opened a tin box.

"*Ah, gute butter* [butter, delicious]. *Danke, Fräulein* [Thank you, young lady]." The soldier smelled the butter, made his friend smell it, closed the tin and put it in the cab of the truck. He handed the tea towel back to Sietske. Johannes and Sietske stared at them.

"*Auf wiedersehen* [Goodbye]." The two soldiers smiled and motioned them to leave. Sietske was the first one to move. Johannes followed and came along beside her.

"The nerve of those two," he said.

"I'm furious," Sietske said. "I wanted to kick both of them in the shins."

Johannes believed she would. "What about your aunt's butter?"

"Oh well, I guess we have to go again some other day." Johannes grinned. He knew Sietske wouldn't give up that easily. "We'll visit her and ask her how much she wants next time," Sietske added. He looked at her. Sietske didn't have an aunt in Franeker. But he had learned not to ask any questions.

They biked downtown. People were dressed in the strangest outfits. An old man wore a paper bag over his head to keep warm. A space was cut out for his eyes and mouth. Some had blankets wrapped around them.

The two bicyclists followed the canal to the west end of the town. With Johannes following close behind, Sietske crossed over a bridge and disappeared into an alley. In front of an old warehouse, she parked her bike against the wall. She signalled Johannes to follow her. A narrow stairway led to a green door on the second floor. Sietske knocked three times.

The door opened and a woman in her late sixties or early seventies answered. Her white hair was tied in a bun. She wore a blue cotton apron over her woollen clothes.

"I'm Sietske Dijkstra. I would like to know how much butter you need and when you want it to be delivered."

"Come in, you two. It is bitterly cold out there. You had a long ride on your bikes."

They followed the woman through a long hallway. Her worn slippers swished over the wooden floor. She opened the door to a room with a round stove in the middle. The steam from a whistling kettle mixed with the smell of burning wood and tobacco. A narrow window provided the only light. Faded red gingham curtains hanging at the sides of the pane framed two red geraniums that sat on the window sill.

"We have visitors, Theunis," the woman said. In the corner of the room sat a man with white, crinkly hair. He looked to be the same age as the woman.

"Here, warm yourselves. You must be frozen." The woman gently pushed Johannes and Sietske towards the stove.

Johannes looked around. A table and two chairs stood in the corner in front of a sink. Two more comfortable chairs and a small coffee table were at the other side of the room. A small dresser with several pictures stood along the wall.

"You'd better give them something hot to drink,"

Theunis said. The woman busied herself with the kettle.

"Who's the young man?" Theunis asked.

"He's my friend and you can trust him," Sietske said.

Johannes felt his cheeks burn. On trial again, he thought. He wondered what would happen if these people found out about his father.

"Does your father know he's come with you?"

"Yes," Sietske said.

The man nodded and eyed Johannes. After a while he said, "I need three pounds of butter for Wednesday night at seven o'clock."

Johannes blinked. How could Theunis know what Sietske had asked the woman? Unless it was some kind of code. Of course it was a code. But what could it mean?

In silence they drank their tea. The warmth from the stove had begun to dry their clothes. Sietske put her cup on the table and walked to the door. Johannes followed. They thanked the woman for the tea.

"Have a safe trip home," she said.

"We tried to bring you some butter today, but the Germans stole it from us," Sietske said.

"The bastards," Theunis growled. "They steal everything they can get their hands on. You're lucky they didn't take your bikes."

They left the building and pedalled back through town.

"I wonder if those two *Moffen* [nickname for the Germans] are still at the water tower," Sietske said. "I'd like to spit at them." She looked at Johannes and started to laugh. "Don't look at me like that. I won't do it."

Johannes grinned. With the wind behind them it didn't feel half as cold, and they had a lot more speed. The army truck was still parked at the water tower. The pair of armed Germans had stopped two old ladies.

"Old ladies and little children are their targets today," Sietske sneered. "Big heroes. I'm sure they will get a medal for this job."

The tallest of the two men spotted them right away. He put his arm up and smiled.

"*Vielen Dank für die Butter* [Thank you for the butter]," he laughed.

Johannes felt helpless and angry. He looked over at Sietske. She turned to the soldiers and stuck out her tongue.

The two Nazis laughed.

They passed. Sietske looked at Johannes. "I couldn't resist," she said.

Johannes grinned. "You always amaze me."

The road was still busy with people from the west walking out in search of food. It was a sad procession of old bikes, homemade carts, wheelbarrows and wagons. The walkers all had tired, hungry faces turned away from the rain and cold.

When Johannes arrived home and entered the stable, Douwe had just started milking the first cow. His father had already done the feeding, which was normally Johannes' job. Ever since his outburst, his father had been quiet. He didn't even scold Johannes for being late.

"Did you see Sietske's aunt?" was all he asked.

"Yes, we visited her and stayed for tea," Johannes answered. He wasn't going to tell him that the Germans had stolen the butter from Sietske or that it hadn't been Sietske's aunt they had visited this afternoon.

# The Plan

By late fall most people had given up hope for a quick liberation. December brought more cold weather to a country that had few resources left for heating. Electricity had been cut off due to a shortage of coal. The pumping stations were all out of order, so water levels rose and large areas became flooded. Food became extremely scarce, especially in the big cities. An endless stream of hungry people knocked on the farm door every day.

Some traded soap or jewellery for food. Others had nothing left to trade. To the annoyance of his father, Johannes' mother tried to give butter and milk to everybody who came to their door. Father was afraid he couldn't deliver enough milk to the Germans. Mother ignored his complaints.

With more frequency the Germans seized cattle for their troops and the people in Germany. Johannes' father organized the transportation of those cattle. Sometimes cows from other farmers were boarded at the van der

Meer farm for a couple of days before being sent off. Since the argument a few weeks ago, his mother never mentioned the cows anymore. Johannes and Sietske also brought food to Johannes' grandparents in the village and to Grandmother van der Meer in Leeuwarden. They'd had no further trouble with German soldiers.

With no electricity and just the one carbide lamp, the evenings were long and boring. Johannes often played board games with Anneke, but his thoughts were elsewhere. He hadn't had too many assignments.

Two weeks before, an attack on the registration office at a neighbouring municipality had been successful. During the night the resistance had walked in, taken food coupons and identity cards and destroyed all the registration cards of the people in the municipality. That wasn't the only raid on registration offices. With so many people in hiding, there was an urgent need for food coupons and identity cards. As a result, all municipal buildings and registration offices now had security guards twenty-four hours a day.

Johannes had not been part of that action. He'd learned about it the next day from Sietske. Sietske's brothers were involved, and probably Minne as well. It was obvious the jobs he was allowed to do were minor and without risk. Were they just to keep him happy? The real work was done by members of the resistance who didn't have a father who was a member of the party. Minne worked at the Dijkstra farm to be close to where the resistance actions were organized.

Two weeks before Christmas, Mother announced, "Grandmother and Grandfather de Boer are moving in to save firewood. It's better that they live here for the winter."

"Where will they stay?" Anneke asked. She worried about giving up her room.

"They can sleep in the front room. We never use it

anyway. We'll move the double bed down from the attic. It's only for a little while. When the cold weather is over, they'll move back to their own house."

Johannes thought about his grandparents. He didn't mind his grandmother so much. She was a quiet person, but Grandfather liked to know everything they did. Hopefully, he wouldn't be too nosy. Johannes liked going his own way, especially now, when he was more involved with Sietske and the resistance.

Two days later his grandparents arrived. Johannes had to bike into the village to help them pack the few belongings they were to bring. They each had a suitcase tied to the back of their bicycles. In his saddlebags, Johannes carried jars with preserved vegetables from his grandparents' summer garden. The wind was biting cold and his grandfather had insisted they wear newspapers under their sweaters. Johannes didn't really want to, but once outside, it was making a difference.

"I'll bike at the front!" Grandfather called. "Grandmother follows me and you have the tail end, Johannes. You young people speed too much for us."

Johannes nodded and took his place at the rear. A tall, skinny man with grey, curly hair, Grandfather de Boer sat straight up on his bike. Behind him followed Grandmother. She was short, her shoulders bent. She suffered from arthritis and her hands had become deformed over the years. Her thin, white hair was tied in a bun and covered with a woollen scarf.

They pedalled over the country roads. Every now and then Grandfather would point to a farm and yell something over his shoulder to Grandmother. On the main road they met many people in search of food. Once they passed a group of children without coats or sweaters, and Johannes saw his grandmother brush tears from her face.

When they arrived at the farm, Mother made substitute coffee and baked some wheat cookies that didn't really taste like anything. Anneke busied herself by helping her grandparents unpack. Grandfather quickly changed into his old work clothes and was ready to help with the milking.

Johannes went to the hayloft to feed the cows. Then he settled into his routine of milking. Just before he finished the second last cow, someone tapped him on the shoulder. Startled, he looked up. It was Sietske. He hadn't heard her enter the stable. She placed her hand on his arm.

"Can you come to the farm tonight at seven?" she whispered.

"Okay," he nodded. "I'll be there." Sietske disappeared as quickly as she had come. He hoped nobody had seen her so he didn't have to explain. Fortunately, since the night his father had lost his temper, he rarely questioned Johannes' comings and goings.

"Who was the pretty young lady sneaking up on you, Johannes?" His grandfather stood right beside him.

Johannes felt his cheeks burn. "It's Sietske from across the bridge. You have met her before, Grandfather."

"Sietske, the little girl who used to race with you on your bikes?" Grandfather asked.

"Yes, that's her."

"She's quite a young lady, Johannes. But why did she sneak up on you like that?"

Johannes sighed. "She is busy helping on their farm, so she didn't have much time, but she wants me to come over tonight." He hoped that would stop the interrogation.

"I don't think you should go out at night, Johannes. The police are becoming really strict after curfew."

"They won't see me, Grandfather," Johannes said. "I don't take the road. I walk through the meadow, cross the bridge and jump the ditch to Dijkstras' farmland."

"Give me the pail, Johannes." Grandfather reached out to take the milk pail from him. "I'd better talk to your father about this. I don't want you to go out."

Johannes walked away to feed the calves. He wished the old man would mind his own business. He wasn't going to stay home for him. Tonight might be important.

During supper that night, the conversation took a wrong turn. Grandfather's voice rose as he said, "That boy has too much freedom. He's only sixteen."

Father nodded and continued to eat.

Mother said, "These are different times than when we grew up, Father. There's nothing for the young people. They can't go out. Dances and parties are forbidden, so what can they do other than visit each other when they get a chance?"

Johannes quickly ate his bread and silently thanked his mother for the speech. She looked up from her plate, her face blank, then winked at him.

Johannes rose from the table. "Don't wait up for me and don't worry about me being seen. I have found the perfect place where I can quickly cross the bridge."

Grandfather's mouth formed a straight, thin line and he frowned under his bushy eyebrows. His father's face showed no emotion. Though her expression was blank, Mother's eyes were smiling.

Johannes hurried over to Sietske's farm and knocked three times on the kitchen window. Sietske opened the door and hugged him quickly. Then she pulled him inside. The kitchen seemed darker than before. The carbide lamp, which normally stood on the table, was gone. Two bicycles fastened on wooden blocks stood on each side of the table. Both bikes were occupied, one by Klaas, the other by Bauke. They were pedalling to keep the lights burning. It was their only source of light tonight.

"We ran out of carbide," Sietske explained. "Tomorrow we'll get more."

"Are you in good shape, Johannes?" Bauke asked. "We have to take turns tonight. We each bike for a half-hour."

"Sure," Johannes said. He looked around the table. Besides Sietske's parents and brothers, there were Minne and another young man. Johannes guessed he was probably in his early twenties. His face was skinny with prominent cheekbones and a pointed chin. Next to him sat an older man, in his late forties or early fifties. His greyish-black hair was unkempt and he hadn't shaved for several days. He wore a navy-blue woollen sweater that was ripped at the neck. Johannes saw no sign of the Jewish family.

"Johannes, this is Willem," Sietske's father pointed to the older man, "and beside him is Jan."

Johannes nodded at both men.

"Sit down. We have to discuss the raid at the distribution office in the village to obtain more food coupons," Bauke said. "This province has become a haven for 'divers' — people in hiding. Since the *Arbeitseinsatz* [forced slave labour], the deportation of Jews, the railroad strike and the closing of the universities, we have had to hide and feed thousands of people."

"Don't forget the American, British and Canadian pilots who have been shot down and rescued," his brother added.

Bauke nodded in agreement. "We hide many Jewish families and downed pilots, as well as students, doctors and lawyers who don't cooperate with the Germans. And since last month, every man between seventeen and fifty-five who doesn't want to work in Germany needs food, a place to stay and a false identity card." He stopped biking and the light in the room turned dim.

Minne took over, and Bauke sat down at the table in Minne's place. He wiped his forehead with the sleeve of his patched, flannel shirt. "Several families in the area are hiding people, and there are not enough food coupons being distributed every month to feed the extra mouths." He looked around the circle of people.

Johannes felt his heart beat faster. Good. Now he was being asked to do some real stuff. Johannes glanced up at Minne. Was that mockery in his old friend's eyes, or was it his imagination?

"This is my plan." Bauke looked around the circle. "Many raids on distribution offices have been successful."

"Not all, Bauke," Willem interrupted, his voice heavy. "The one from last week was discovered. The security police threw seven of our members in jail."

Bauke cleared his throat. "I know, Willem. But we are not here to discuss the actions that go wrong. Tomorrow night before curfew, we'll raid our municipality office. Two at a time, we'll travel to the village. At seven o'clock some of you will meet at the back of the local office. Make sure you're not seen. Jan and Willem will go inside the building."

"What about the two security guards?" Willem asked.

"You and Jan have to take care of them," Bauke answered. "They usually sit in the front office. Jan is an expert in taking out windows. Make sure you wear your masks and put socks over your shoes. I'll give you enough rope to tie up the guards. Use your weapons only as a last resort. Jan knows where they keep the food coupons, and he will fill several bags." Bauke looked at Jan. The younger man nodded. "Minne will be posted outside. Willem and Minne will take the bags from Jan. Then they'll bring them to the old shack behind the building. At seven-twenty my father and Klaas will pick up the bags. They'll have to hide them under their clothing and will leave the shack separately, ten minutes apart. Everybody got that so far?"

Johannes' spirits sank. Where did he come in? He chewed on his bottom lip and shifted his feet under the table.

"Father and Klaas will get the address of where to deliver the loot from Willem," Bauke continued. "I'll tell him as soon as I have confirmed my contact place. Johannes, your job is to warn Willem if anybody enters the building or if there are Germans in the area. You tap on the window at the rear of the building. Your hiding place is behind the shrubs at the side of the office. You'll have a good view of the main road and the bridge. You and Sietske will bicycle to the farm beside the drawbridge. Sietske will stay at the farm. You'll leave your bike there. You'll walk unnoticed to the building. At seven-thirty, you'll return to the farm. Then, you and Sietske will pedal home."

"And if things go wrong?" Johannes asked.

"You disappear unnoticed," Bauke answered.

Johannes looked over at Sietske. She smiled at him warmly. He wasn't sure what to think. Did he have the least risky job?

"Johannes can wear his normal clothes. Everybody else bring your mask and a revolver. Okay? Are there any questions?"

"Yes," Willem said as he stood up. "How can we be sure that the son of a collaborator is not going to leak our little plan?"

Johannes felt as if the man had slapped him in the face. How did Willem know? He had never seen the man before. Bauke must have informed him. So this was the test? To see if he could be trusted?

He pulled himself together, rose, looked Willem straight in the eye and said, "You just have to trust me."

"What guarantees do we have that you won't betray us?" Willem's dark eyes bored into him.

"There are no guarantees. This is war," Johannes answered. "I'll be here tomorrow night at six-fifteen."

Sietske walked Johannes to the door. In the hallway he turned around. "Don't come out with me tonight."

She clutched his sleeve. "Johannes, don't be angry. Can't you understand? These people are risking their lives. They don't know you."

"I do understand, but I am angry. Who told him about my father? I hate Willem. Who does he think he is? Good night. I'll see you tomorrow."

He opened the door and walked into the ice-cold night.

# The Raid

"Mother, I need to go to Sietske's early tonight. Please, just for once, will you feed the calves for me?" Johannes whispered.

She seized his arms, her eyes glistening. "Whatever you're up to, Johannes, please be careful." She let go of him and turned her head away.

"Don't worry, Mother. I . . . ah . . . do farm work. They are short-handed." He hated lying to his mother, but he couldn't bear her pained expression.

"Leave quickly, so Grandfather doesn't have any questions."

"But he will have questions for you, Mother," Johannes said.

"I'll tell him what you told me," she answered. "Now, hurry."

Johannes dressed warmly, and quietly went out through the laundry room into the darkness. The evening air was bitterly cold. The moon and the stars were hidden by heavy clouds. He'd managed to take his bicycle out of the barn before milking time and had parked it against the side of the house. With the bike under his arm, he quickly made his way to the meadow. At the main road, he decided to ride the short distance to Sietske's farm. He saw the odd person with a wagon or a cart, but most people had already found a place to stay for the night.

Sietske met him at the end of her driveway. With a knitted wool toque over her ears and a scarf covering her nose and mouth, he hardly recognized her.

"Ready?" she asked.

"Yes, let's go. Did the others leave yet?"

"I don't know," she said. "Bauke said to leave as soon as you arrived."

They pedalled in silence for a while. Their two bike lights seemed to be the only beacons in the dark evening. Presently they turned off the main road and followed the street along the canal.

"Sietske?"

"Yes?"

"What happened to Natalie and her family?"

"They're gone," Sietske answered. "Remember how we visited my Aunt Siet and Theunis the other day? They asked for three pounds of butter for Wednesday night at seven?"

"Yes, I remember," Johannes said. "That didn't make much sense to me. I thought it was some kind of a code."

"You were right," Sietske said. "On the Wednesday night, Minne and I went with the horse and wagon into Franeker. We had to deliver boxes with furniture to the warehouse you and I had visited two days before. Beneath the boxes, the Jewish family was hidden. The wagon had an extra space underneath the floor planks."

"You and Minne!" Johannes' mouth fell open. "That was very dangerous! How could your father send you and Minne!" Johannes bristled with fury. He halted and dismounted. Sietske followed suit and stood beside her bike, facing him.

"It seemed safer if we did the job than any of the older boys or my father!" Sietske's voice had risen, too.

"I can't believe you did it. What if the Germans had stopped you and had found those people?"

"Well, they didn't. I wish I had never told you. I don't know why you're angry. Is it because Minne was with me? Or because you didn't get the job?"

"You figure it out!" he snapped back. He turned, mounted his bicycle and rode ahead of her. He didn't care if she couldn't keep up, although the squeaking of her old bike told him she wasn't far behind.

They entered the village and met two army trucks. Johannes slowed down and waited for Sietske to catch up to him.

"Sorry," he said.

She didn't respond. Turning left over the drawbridge, they were met at the farm by an old German shepherd. The dog barked, then came over to lick their hands.

"He knows you're good folks," came a voice from the barn door. "Come inside."

Johannes and Sietske followed the farmer into the warmth of the barn. His back bent, the old man walked slowly in front of them. A soft, yellow light shone from a storm lamp he carried in his hand. Hay stuck out of his wooden shoes, to keep his feet warm.

"This cold weather doesn't agree with my joints," he said. "You stay here with me in the stable, young lady, and you, young man," he pointed to Johannes, "you have a job to do."

"Yes, I'd better go now." Johannes left the barn. He looked around, but no one was out if they didn't have to be. He crossed the bridge and followed the left side of the road, the same side as the municipal office. Passing the building, he turned around and peered into the dark. He couldn't see a thing, only sky and the dark outline of the structure. The windows had been covered with blackout curtains. He turned around and quickly disappeared behind the bushes on the right side of the building.

He shivered. When his eyes adjusted to the dark, he could make out the contours of the bridge. Across the street, someone was walking a dog. He hoped the animal wouldn't smell him or choose these bushes for his favourite stop. Even though the Germans had forbidden the cutting of trees, it was amazing how many trees and telephone poles were missing, vanished during the night. People needed firewood.

Johannes settled down and kept his eyes on the bridge and the road ahead. He had no idea what time it was. The darkness made it impossible to read his watch. All he could do was wait for the chimes in the church tower. Two years before, the Nazis had stolen all the church bells and taken them to Germany to be melted down in the factories. The people had been outraged, but they had created their own church bells. Empty air tanks or parts of steel railroad tracks were now used to chime the hour and half-hour in the villages and towns.

A car drove toward him. Johannes held his breath. The auto drove away over the drawbridge. He exhaled in relief.

Before long the church clock chimed seven. Now the operation would begin. He strained his ears to hear noises coming from the back of the building, but heard not a sound. These men must have executed break-ins before. They knew exactly where to be and how to work efficiently. His heart pounded. Use your guns only as a last resort, Bauke had said. Johannes would be able to hear any gunfire, but many others would, too.

So far not a sound had escaped the walls. He wondered if the two security guards had been tied up yet. They were often party members, just like his father. He hoped his father didn't engage in security operations, although whatever activities his father was involved in were probably just as dangerous.

It started to snow. This weather didn't help. Johannes wished they would hurry up. He still had to wait for the seven-thirty chime. He wondered if Minne was in his spot behind the building. His friend probably didn't trust him any more than Willem did. Some gut feeling told Johannes that he had to watch out for Willem, although he couldn't explain why.

Another car headed toward him. It aimed straight for the building, slowed, then stopped. Johannes froze.

On his haunches, he eased backwards. He stood up, dashed behind the building and crashed right into someone. It was Minne.

"Disappear! There's a car in front of the building," Johannes panted.

"Go back." Minne shoved him. "Come and get us when it's safe."

Johannes stayed close to the wall. He fell on his knees just as two beams of light came around the building. As he slid down onto his stomach, he wished the lights would go away. Two men stood on the road, shining their flashlights up and down the building. To Johannes, it seemed like ages before they finally left. On his stomach, he slithered along the ground until he reached the bushes. The car was parked in front of the building. He could hear the men's voices. They sounded German. Finally the two men got back into their car. The vehicle backed up and turned left over the drawbridge.

Johannes sighed. As soon as the car disappeared, he got up and ran to the rear of the building. He knocked on the window. Someone opened it from the inside. Jan stuck his head out.

"Johannes?"

"Yes, they're gone."

"Okay, grab this bag and take it to the shack. Tell them it's safe. Then go back to your spot. Good work, Johannes."

"Thanks." Johannes felt better. He reached for the bag Jan handed him through the open window. He hurried down to an old wooden shack, which couldn't be seen from the road. He knocked three times.

"Who is it?" He recognized Willem's voice.

"It's Johannes. The Germans are gone." Willem opened the door and Johannes handed him the bag. Without a word, he hurried back to his hiding place and waited. It was snowing harder now. Fat, wet flakes were accumulating on his hat and shoulders. His legs felt wet through his pants. The minutes passed like hours.

A soft rustling sound startled him. He didn't have time to turn before someone jumped him from behind.

"Ah!" A hand covered his mouth before his cry could alert the neighbourhood. "I got you, Johannes," Willem sneered. "I just wanted to see how alert you were." He let go of Johannes, then vanished in the dark.

Johannes fell onto his knees and covered his face with his hands. So this was Willem's way of testing new members of the resistance. He'd never been so startled and scared. What a mean trick! Well, he wouldn't tell anybody. That wouldn't stop Willem from getting satisfaction over his bad joke, as Willem could and probably would tell everyone himself.

When the half-hour chimed, Johannes got up and went around the building one last time. The window had been closed and there was no sign of the men. He let two bicyclists pass by before he left his hiding place and started back to the farm. Wet snow slapped his face as he crossed the drawbridge. The German shepherd barked a greeting at the stable. A faint light spread across the floor.

Sietske sprang up from a bench. "Are you safe, Johannes?" He heard the trembling in her voice.

"I wouldn't be here if I wasn't," he answered.

"I know. I mean, was the operation a success?"

"I hope so, but I only did my part. I don't know what happened to the rest of the men. Let's go home. I'm frozen."

Sietske dressed in her blanket coat and scarf. They quietly took their bikes and left the stable. There was no sign of the old farmer. The snow fell more heavily on the way home. Johannes had never felt so cold. Even his bones felt frozen. They kept their eyes on the road, but the falling snow made visibility poor. Johannes didn't say much. The cold had even numbed his feelings. Sietske glanced at him several times, but she kept silent.

All at once, the sky lit up in the east. Searchlights beamed across, ready to spot Allied planes.

"We'd better hurry," he said. "It might be a long night if the bombers come this soon."

At the Dijkstras' driveway they stopped. "I can go the rest of the way alone," Sietske said in a flat voice. "You'd better change into dry clothes or you'll get sick. I'll see you." She aimed her bike towards home and disappeared.

Johannes would have liked to know if the others had returned yet and if the raid had been successful, but his need for shelter and warmth took over. He hurried home. He'd just moved his bike inside the barn when the sirens began their familiar blaring.

"Damn!" He wanted nothing more than to get into dry clothes and go to bed, but the family all had to go into the shelter. If he didn't show up, he could just imagine his grandfather's questions and his father's sad expression.

# Bicycle Thieves

During the week before Christmas, Johannes had to deliver food coupons to several addresses in town. Usually he went alone. It seemed Sietske did more dangerous work these days; often she worked with Minne. Johannes was forced to admit to himself that he was jealous.

The resistance's raid on the local government building had been a success. There hadn't been any bloodshed. They had taken enough food coupons to feed people in outlying areas for a month. No retaliation had been taken by the Germans, although security had been tightened at municipal offices.

Other actions by the resistance had been less successful, and the retribution by the Germans was brutal. In the town of Dokkum, an attack on two Nazi officers had led to the torture and execution of twenty political prisoners.

At home, Johannes helped Douwe cut trees. It hurt him to see the large poplars crash to the ground, but to keep warm they needed to cut down every tree on the property.

"We have started to take the shelves out of the cupboards," Douwe said. "I'll saw the planks into small square pieces tonight. When the shelves are finished, I guess we'll have to take out the bedroom doors and burn those."

"You can take home the branches from this tree," Johannes said. "There are enough logs left for my family."

He'd put down his axe and watched the older man gather up the branches. "Do you still listen to the BBC at night Douwe?"

"Yes. We never miss it."

"What's the latest news about the progress of the Allied troops?"

"There is no progress." Douwe sat down on a stump. He put the branches on the ground and wiped his face with his glove. "The Germans have a strong tank division to defend the bridges. The Canadians and the British don't have the proper equipment nor enough men to cross the river."

"And where are the Americans?" Johannes asked eagerly.

"They're fighting in Belgium in the Ardennes."

They were silent. Johannes looked at the stump-covered orchard. Mother wouldn't be able to cook any more homemade applesauce, his favourite food.

"The best news lately is that the R.A.F.'s nighttime weapons drop is going very well. The resistance is stocking up on different guns and ammunition." Slowly, Douwe rose from the stump. He took his branches and trudged around to the stable.

Johannes picked up some of the twigs and broke them into short sticks. He carried the load of kindling inside. At the kitchen door he stopped.

"You should never have signed up!" Grandfather's deep voice was higher than normal. "You will regret it when the war is over!"

"It's not as bad as you see it." His father's voice was

calm. "I agree I don't like taking cows and food from the farmers, but I'm a member. I have no choice."

A sickening feeling sank in Johannes' stomach. He leaned his head against the wall.

"Help your party friends and betray your fellow countrymen!" Grandfather shouted. "You're hiding behind your pride, Durk. Don't pretend you don't know what's really going on. You know damn well what the Germans are up to."

"I haven't betrayed anybody," his father answered hoarsely. "We'd better stop arguing before we both say something we can't take back. We can't agree on this anyway."

"Don't you have your doubts, Durk? I must admit that in the beginning of the war I didn't think it would be all that bad. But now we all know the dirty work the Germans do. We know what they do to Jewish people, to political prisoners and to all those men who have been sent to work in the German factories. What about your conscience?"

"I don't want to talk about it." Father's voice shook.

"Why can't you admit you've made a mistake? Is that so difficult?"

"It's too late to back down," Father answered.

"Admit you've made a mistake. For the sake of my daughter! For your children!" Grandfather's voice quavered. "You have responsibilities toward your country, your family!"

"I better get to work."

Johannes opened the door. His eyes moved from his father to his grandfather. They didn't speak. His father stared at him and Johannes' cheeks burned. He busied himself with the kindling. Without a word, Father left the kitchen. Mother and Grandmother had both been quietly knitting. He could see how painful the knitting was for his grandmother's hands. Mother was the first one to speak up.

"I wish you would stop arguing, Father. I would like to have some peace in this family. We have to live under the same roof."

"Yes, you're right," he said.

"I wish I could change Durk's beliefs. I've tried, Father, believe me. And now . . . " Mother looked at the clock on the mantel. A single tear rolled down her cheek. "I've given up," she said in a thick voice.

Johannes swallowed. Why did his father have to hurt everybody?

"You look tired, Nynke," Grandfather spoke gently. "You should look after yourself." He walked over and patted his daughter gently on the shoulder.

"Don't worry about me." She quickly composed herself and smiled at Johannes. "Will you meet Anneke at school, Johannes? It is so cold today, I can't help but worry about her. And while you're in the village, could the two of you drop off some wool for Minne's mother?"

Johannes looked surprised. "Yes, sure." Maybe he would have a chance to talk to his friend's mother. He hadn't realized his mother was still in contact with her. He smiled at the thought.

With a bag of wool and five pairs of knitted socks in his saddlebags, and dressed as if he were on his way to the North Pole, Johannes rode off. The wind was behind him, so he entered the village quickly. The street to the school was crowded with people.

He could hear one woman screaming, "You think I'd give up my silver tea set? Never! It was a wedding present from my mother!"

At the end of the street stood an army truck. Soldiers were going door to door. Johannes stopped at the school and watched the action in the street. An old man came to stand beside him.

"What's going on?" Johannes asked.

"The Germans are seizing copper and tin items

again. They melt them in the factories to make more bullets." He spit a wad of tobacco on the ground. "My wife has hidden all her stuff in a secret place. They'll never find it," he grinned.

"But what if they do?" Johannes asked.

"They'll get shit all over them. Ha, ha, ha."

"You mean she put it in the outhouse?"

"Yes, right down in the you-know-what."

The school bell rang and Anneke came through the door, the hood of her oversized winter coat covering half her face. Johannes waved. When she spotted him, her face brightened.

"Good luck," he said to the old man. Anneke picked up her bike. They didn't stay for the action in the street.

"How come you're here?" she said.

"Mother asked me to pick you up. We have to take some wool to Minne's mother."

"That's my job," Anneke said. "I always take stuff to Minne's mother. But Father is not to know about it. Actually, nobody is to know about it," she said proudly.

Johannes swallowed. So the underground movement was right under his nose, in his own house, and he didn't know about it. "I must admit, you and Mother are a great team," he said. "What is Mrs. de Jong's role?"

"Mrs. de Jong helps the families of political prisoners and the families whose fathers and sons have to work in Germany in the factories," Anneke said. They turned onto the street to Minne's house. Anneke parked her bike against the fence and knocked at the door. Johannes saw the lace curtain of the kitchen window move. A few seconds later the door opened.

"Come inside, you two," Mrs. de Jong said. "I can't believe how cold it is."

They stepped into the small hallway, where they left their wooden shoes before entering the kitchen.

"Here, sit close to the stove. I can hardly heat the

kitchen enough to make it comfortable," she said. "I'll warm up some milk for you."

"No, thank you," Johannes and Anneke said at the same time. "You keep the milk," Johannes added. "We have enough at home."

On the mantel stood a large photograph of Minne's father. Mrs. de Jong followed Johannes' gaze. "He doesn't have to suffer anymore," she said hoarsely. She turned around and stared out the window.

"Minne's at the Dijkstras' farm?" Johannes asked awkwardly.

Mrs. de Jong nodded.

"We'd better be on our way. Soon it will be milking time again." Johannes stood up and Anneke followed.

"Thank your mother for the wool and the warm socks," Mrs. de Jong said. As she opened the door for them, a gust of northern wind blew inside. Wrestling with the door, she closed it quickly behind them.

Johannes and Anneke pedalled to the end of the village.

"Look, Johannes," said Anneke. "Another German truck is blocking the road. I'm so glad you're with me today. Do you think they'll stop us?"

"Don't panic," Johannes said. "We have nothing to hide."

Slowly they biked toward the truck. Johannes felt his temper rising. Sure, he thought, those stupid Nazis sit inside, out of the weather, while we are out here.

Two soldiers in black uniforms jumped out of the cab.

"*Halt! Absteigen* [Stop! Dismount]!"

Johannes and Anneke both stepped down. Anneke gasped as one of the men grabbed her bike. Johannes moved toward his sister.

"*Halt!*" The soldier pointed his rifle at Johannes.

Johannes froze. Anneke's eyes opened wide and her hand moved to her mouth. Holding the rifle in one hand and Anneke's bicycle in the other, the soldier stared at Johannes. His friend walked over and calmly took away Johannes' bike.

"*Auf wiedersehen* [Goodbye]," he said. He loaded Johannes' bike onto the back of the truck. Anneke's followed. Then he lowered his gun and the two Nazis climbed into the cab.

"Let's go." Johannes took Anneke's hand. "We better walk home fast. It's freezing cold." They walked briskly in the cold winter afternoon.

"You were brave, Anneke." Johannes looked down at his sister's pale face.

"No, I was scared. Were you?"

"Yes," Johannes answered. "I wonder what Father will say?"

A black Mercedes stood parked in the driveway when they got home.

"It's *Herr* Obermann and his gang," Anneke said. "I hope they aren't in the house."

"They usually stay in the stable," Johannes said.

The door opened before them. "Where are your bikes?" Mother asked.

"Stolen by some German heroes with a big rifle," Johannes answered angrily.

"You'd better tell your father. At least the two of you are safe," she said.

Johannes dressed for milking and walked into the stable. His father looked up and came over to him.

"Our bicycles were stolen by your friends." Johannes pointed at the two Nazis who stood at the other end of the stable.

"Shh. Watch your big mouth. You can start milking immediately. Your mother will help you. I have to go out."

Johannes nodded. It was going to be a long evening. Douwe's hands were stiff with arthritis, and his grandfather wasn't much help, either.

"You don't have to do this," he said to his mother as she entered the stable, her eyes full of exhaustion. "Anneke can help with the calves. Oh, and she shouldn't go to school by herself. Our experience this afternoon scared her."

"Yes, boss," his mother smiled.

Later that evening after supper, when Johannes and Anneke were playing a game of cards, his grandfather reading a book and the two women knitting socks, his father returned from town . . . with their bikes.

No questions asked.

# The English Pilot

Christmas came and went, and Anneke complained how boring it was. With a regular Sunday and Christmas Day followed by Boxing Day, there were three Sundays in a row with little to do. Mother had tried her best to make a special meal for Christmas Day. The Christmas pudding looked delicious, but tasted like boiled flour batter. Anneke and Mother had gone to church in the afternoon, and Johannes had visited Sietske. Something had changed in their relationship. Sietske kept her distance and so did he. They had listened to the BBC radio broadcasting a Christmas concert. Even with static interference, peace on earth sounded beautiful.

The cold weather continued. Night temperatures fell below zero. Ditches, canals and flooded pastures froze. Many people made use of the new iceways to skate from village to village. Even some people who were in hiding couldn't resist and borrowed skates.

The Germans became more unreasonable as they lost ground at the Eastern front. Five political prisoners were shot for no other reason than to set an example and create fear.

Nazi commanders from Belgium and the southern parts of the Netherlands were stationed in the north. Their reputation for cruelty was worse than those of the German SS. The commander of the town of Heerenveen openly stated that he hated the Friesian people. "They are stubborn, proud and loyal to their queen," he said. "It is impossible to break their spirits. Therefore, I want to see as many dead Friesians as possible."

As the days grew longer in January, people became a little more optimistic. The war had to end soon. Halifax planes from the R.A.F. dropped weapons for the resistance almost every night. The resistance took more risks, but in their desperation the Germans' retaliation became more and more severe. For every German killed by the resistance, ten political prisoners were executed.

Often Johannes spent Wednesday nights at the Dijkstra farm, listening to the radio or receiving information from Bauke. He still braved small jobs for the resistance. But it bothered him that Minne continued to work on bigger, more risky operations.

Johannes wished his grandparents would return to their own home. With his father gone most nights, Grandfather made everything his business, as if he owned the farm. Johannes tried not to say anything. Often, he noticed his mother, too, had great difficulty keeping her mouth closed.

One night, when Johannes was crossing the bridge to the other side of Sietske's farm, the searchlights from the air base began to comb the sky. One plane flew low over the farm buildings. He heard the anti-aircraft guns. His eyes tried to follow the plane. The aircraft was small in size, maybe a Spitfire. A sudden flash hit the plane. Then he heard a loud explosion. In the glare from the burning plane, Johannes thought he saw the pilot jump out. He ran to the farm and knocked three times on the window.

"Quick, come outside!" Johannes yelled. "An Allied plane has crashed. The pilot might still be alive!"

He heard footsteps running to the door. "Johannes?" Bauke came outside, followed by Klaas and Sietske. "We didn't realize it was a plane. We heard the impact and assumed it was a bomb." He turned to Sietske and Klaas. "Dress warmly." He ran back into the kitchen and called out, "Mother, take out the first-aid box and get the shelter ready. We might have a wounded visitor tonight."

Mr. Dijkstra came to the door. "I'd better stay here in case we get more visitors. Hurry up. Find him before the Germans get their hands on him."

The four of them ran south, toward the pink glow.

"He might have crashed into the canal," Bauke said.

They ran and stumbled across the fields until they reached the canal. The bright glow was gone. The four crept along the reeds. The canal was frozen. They could see dark water where the ice had been broken. The smell of gasoline penetrated their nostrils. Smoke pricked their eyes.

"Shine your flashlight along the reeds," Klaas whispered.

"I hate to make any light at all," Bauke answered. "The Germans might be here at any time."

"There." Sietske stepped forward. "It's the plane."

Before them, something dark loomed. It seemed to be in the shape of a wing. Fortunately, the bottom of the canal was shallow. There was enough water to extinguish the flames, but not enough to swallow up the whole plane.

Bauke stopped. "It's a Spitfire. So we look for one person. Klaas and Johannes, you two cross the ice and check the other side of the canal for the pilot. Sietske and I will take this side. Whistle three times if you find him."

Johannes followed Klaas to a place where the ice seemed strong enough to support them. "Stay low," Klaas whispered. They both bent and slid across the ice to the other side. "Could you see which side of the plane he jumped out?"

"West of the burning plane," Johannes answered. They followed the reeds to the west, staying low.

Johannes tripped over something and fell flat on his face. Instead of sharp reeds, his skin felt fabric. Klaas helped him back onto his feet. He rubbed his knees, which had hit the frozen earth.

"It's the parachute," Klaas exclaimed. "He must be close by."

Johannes untangled himself from the material and the strings.

"Here!" Klaas called. "I've found him."

Johannes quickly followed the direction of Klaas' voice. He found Klaas bent over a body.

"Is he dead?" Johannes asked.

"I think he's unconscious. I can feel a pulse, but I can't tell if he has any broken bones. Let's fold the parachute into a makeshift stretcher."

Johannes scrambled back to get the parachute. "Turn on your flashlight, Klaas, so I can see what I'm doing."

Klaas shone the beam from the flashlight low to the ground while they made the stretcher. Carefully, they lifted the pilot onto it. A moan escaped his lips. They folded the fabric around him.

"Let's carry him across the ice," Klaas said. "Then, we'll whistle for the others. I'll take the front. Tell me when I go too fast."

"All right," Johannes said. He held the makeshift stretcher with both hands.

Klaas moved onto the ice. "Lower him, Johannes. We can pull him. It will be faster."

On the other side of the canal, they lifted up the pilot and waded through the reeds. Klaas whistled three times. Within seconds, Bauke and Sietske appeared.

"We found him and made a stretcher out of his

parachute," Klaas told the others.

"Great work," Bauke answered. "We don't want to leave the parachute behind. We can't stay here any longer. We must all take turns carrying him, except for Sietske."

Sietske opened her mouth to protest, but her brother cut her off.

Slowed down by the weight of the patient on the stretcher, the small troop of rescuers stumbled home. The uneven ground, the darkness and the cold northern wind made their trip difficult. Even though the three young men took turns carrying the stretcher, it seemed like hours before they at last reached the farm.

"Sietske, walk alongside the wall to the front of the house and warn us if we have any visitors," Bauke said. "We will stay in the ditch behind the barn."

Johannes couldn't help but admire Bauke. He thought of every detail and didn't take unnecessary risks.

The pilot started to moan. "You are safe," Bauke spoke to him in English. "We will help you."

"The fire?" the pilot asked in a shaky voice.

"Yes, your plane caught fire when it was hit by anti-aircraft fire."

"Yes," the man answered. He stopped talking and groaned with pain.

"It's safe." Sietske returned from her scouting assignment. "Father will help us into the barn. The pilot has to be taken straight to the hiding place. You have to tell him to be very still. The Germans are certain to search the area tonight. Bauke and Klaas, you have to make sure he is warm enough. Mother has brought food and milk for him to the shelter. As soon as the pilot is in hiding, you have to go to the kitchen. We can't look after his wounds now. Johannes, come with me." She grabbed Johannes' sleeve.

"But I have to help carry the pilot inside," Johannes protested.

Nobody spoke.

He looked from Bauke to Klaas. "Fine." He got the hint. He wasn't allowed to know the hiding place. They still didn't trust him. He sighed and followed Sietske to the house, while her brothers took the pilot into the barn. Before he entered, Johannes turned to look back. He could see Mr. Dijkstra pointing a flashlight to guide the small group inside.

The kitchen felt warm and cozy. The smell of wood mingled with heated milk filled his nostrils. Wodan was asleep beside the stove in his wicker basket.

"Here, some hot milk to warm your insides." Mrs. Dijkstra poured the steaming milk into glasses and placed them in front of the two. Johannes warmed his hands around the glass. The heat penetrated his hands and arms.

"I wish the others would come inside." Mrs. Dijkstra's voice quavered. She brushed the hair away from her forehead. "You two should play something," she said, as she reached for a board and a box with chess pieces. "Pretend you are in the middle of the game."

Johannes and Sietske placed half the chess pieces on the board.

"I'd like to win this game," Sietske laughed, to break the tension. Johannes looked at her, filled with admiration.

The kitchen door swung open and the three men walked inside and quickly hung up their coats. Mr. Dijkstra warmed his hands above the woodstove while Mrs. Dijkstra poured more milk and gave each of them a book to open.

"How is he?" she asked.

"Not too bad," her husband answered. "He might have a concussion and some broken ribs. His one ankle's swollen, but other than that, he seems grateful to be safe and alive."

"How old?" his wife asked.

"A young boy — perhaps early twenties."

Sietske's mother sighed and shook her head. Johannes wondered if her thoughts were with the boy's parents.

The clock ticked peacefully. They'd all gathered around the table. Mrs. Dijkstra's knitting needles clicked an even rhythm and the dreaming cat in front of the stove twitched his whiskers. Once in a while another piece was moved across the chess board. Wodan snored lightly.

Screeching tires in the gravel outside broke the fragile peace inside the kitchen. The dog jumped up and barked. The sound of car doors opening and closing was followed by the tramping of heavy boots coming to the house and the pounding of a fist against the door.

"*Aufmachen* [Open up]!"

"I'll go." Mrs. Dijkstra wiped her hands on her apron and walked to the hallway to open the door. Mr. Dijkstra called Wodan to sit beside him. Everyone in the kitchen held their breath.

A commander of the security police and two soldiers marched into the kitchen. Johannes' chest felt tight. His hands clamped into fists under the table. Sietske looked right at the soldiers. Mr. Dijkstra, Bauke and Klaas didn't seem to be at all frightened.

"*Guten Abend* [Good evening]," the commander said. He looked around the table to see if he recognized one of the faces.

"*Um ungefähr sieben Uhr heute abend ist ein Flugzeug abgestürzt. Haben sie etwas gehört oder gesehen* [A plane crashed tonight at about seven o'clock. Did you see or hear anything]?"

"*Ja, wir haben eine Explosion gehört* [Yes, we heard an explosion]," Bauke answered. "*Wir dachten es war eine Bombe* [We thought it was a bomb]."

The commander looked hard at each of them. Johannes and the others returned his gaze. The buttons on the soldiers' uniforms shone in the dim light. Their rifles gleamed. The smell of their polished leather boots filled the kitchen. Wodan growled and bared his teeth. Sietske's father held him by the collar.

The commander nodded. *"Wir müssen das Haus und die Ställe durch suchen* [We have to search the house and the farm]."

Johannes felt his nails digging in his flesh.

"Yes," Mr. Dijkstra nodded.

One of the soldiers eyed the dog nervously. Wodan seemed to feel the anxiety of the man. He strained to get to him. In a flash, the Nazi pointed his gun at the dog.

Sietske's father rose from his chair and faced the soldier head on. The Nazi lowered his gun. Johannes wrung his hands under the table. Underneath his warm sweater he felt cold sweat chill his back.

The commander turned his flashlight on. *"Du, mitkommen* [You, come with us]!" He pointed to Bauke.

Bauke stood up calmly and followed the men to the bedrooms and the front room. Nobody spoke. They could hear doors and drawers being opened. Johannes wondered what they expected to find in the drawers. Certainly no pilot.

After what seemed like hours, they came back through the kitchen. Bauke opened the door to the stable. The soldiers stepped through first. Before Bauke closed the door, he winked at Sietske.

Johannes looked around the room. No one showed any expression. They all seemed very calm. Sietske's father had seated himself again and so had the dog, although he looked alert, his ears stiffly upright.

"Don't worry. They'll never find him," Sietske whispered.

Johannes wasn't so sure, but he nodded. The clock ticked. The kettle on the stove whistled softly and Johannes' heart beat a mile a minute.

The sound of boots returned to the kitchen, and everyone shifted in their seats. Wodan rose and began to bark, but Mr. Dijkstra quietly restrained him and stroked his neck. The commander walked in first. Again he studied their faces. He was a tall, well-built man with a stern, but not unfriendly face. The soldiers and Bauke followed.

"*Wir kommen morgen wieder. Vielleicht könnt ihr uns helfen. Es ist zu kalt und zu dunkel draußen* [We'll come back in the morning. Perhaps you can help us. It is too cold and too dark outside]," the commander said. He scanned the table once more.

They nodded slightly.

"*Guten Abend* [Good night]," he said, and left the kitchen. The two German soldiers followed him.

They heard the front door close. Outside, car doors opened and slammed shut. The engine revved. Tires crunched on the gravel as the car sped away. They all listened till the sound of the engine disappeared.

"Johannes, you'd better go home now." Mrs. Dijkstra broke the silence.

"What will happen to the pilot?" he questioned.

"He'll be safe and well looked after," Bauke said. "By tomorrow he'll be gone. Thank you, Johannes. You did an excellent job."

Johannes felt good, but knew his job was finished. They didn't need him anymore. He wasn't fully included in the resistance operations. The thought stabbed him. But he was glad he had helped rescue the pilot. For the first time, he had felt useful.

Sietske walked him to the door. He pulled on his winter gear.

"You were wonderful tonight, Johannes." She pecked him on the cheek.

He looked into her warm eyes. "So were you, and the rest of your family."

As he walked home, he wished he, too, could be proud of every member of his family.

# Captured

"Johannes!" Surprised, he looked up. He'd just cut down the last plum tree, Mother's favourite. Sietske came running towards him. Johannes almost lost his balance when she threw herself at him.

"Oh, Johannes," she sobbed.

Johannes slipped his arms around her and held her close. "Tell me what has happened," he urged.

"Not here." Her face was red and swollen. "Let's walk."

He left the axe on the stump of the plum tree. "We'll walk along the canal." Johannes tucked Sietske's hand with his inside his coat pocket. Her breathing quietened as they stepped away from the farm. He didn't say anything until she was ready to talk.

"Last night the provincial leader of the resistance, Inspector Bakker, was caught by the Germans. They kept him overnight in a small police station in Sneek."

Johannes pressed her arm gently. He was relieved that she was willing to share this information with him, but at the same time his heart was filled with apprehension.

"The resistance has tapped the police station telephone. Some members listened in on the conversations and found out exactly when Inspector Bakker would be transported to the House of Detention in Leeuwarden."

"I can't believe the people in the resistance have access to so much information!" Johannes exclaimed.

Sietske ignored his outburst. "Last night a plan was made to free the leader on his way to Leeuwarden. This morning at ten-thirty, ten resistance members blocked the road just outside Sneek and attacked the car that held the inspector."

"Who was involved?" Johannes was suddenly full of fear. He looked over at Sietske. She had trouble speaking. Fresh tears welled up in her eyes. "Let's sit down."

"No, I'd rather keep walking," she said. The reeds along the canal shuddered. The ice gleamed in the pale light of the day.

She shivered. "By now you've realized this morning's action failed. The setup was perfect, but they weren't lucky today. An army truck full of soldiers arrived from the opposite direction. Our men had no chance." She stopped again.

"Did someone leak the plan?" he asked.

"No, Bauke doesn't think so. The army truck came at the wrong time. At the wrong spot. I couldn't warn them. They seemed to arrive out of nowhere."

"You were there?" he gasped. "Bauke involved you in a dangerous action like this?"

"I wanted to be involved. I had a good hiding spot."

He couldn't believe it. He didn't want her involved in such operations. "Don't blame yourself, Sietske." Johannes slipped his arm around her shoulder, but she pushed him away.

"I don't. But I couldn't do anything, and now Klaas, Minne and six other people are in jail. Only Bauke and Willem escaped."

"Oh, Sietske. What do we do now?"

"That's the reason I'm here. Will you help us, Johannes?"

"Of course I will. Did you think I wouldn't?"

"Our next job will not be easy," she said. "And it will be dangerous. Are you willing to risk your life for your friend and my brother?" She stopped and turned to look him straight in the face.

He stared into her dark eyes. "Are you willing to risk your life?" he whispered.

"Yes," she said in a firm voice.

He looked away. Then, turning back to her, he said, "I am, too." Their eyes held. Slowly Johannes bent his head, wrapped both arms around her and kissed her forehead.

Sietske pulled away first. "You'll have to come to Leeuwarden with me. We have to get some bread at the bakery across from the House of Detention."

"The House of Detention?"

"Yes," Sietske answered. "The place where all political prisoners are kept. If the Germans make them talk, Johannes, a lot of people will lose their lives. We might be detained, too. I won't go back to the farm with you. I'll follow the canal and cross the bridge at your secret pathway. Meet me in half an hour at my driveway. If you can't get away, I'll go alone."

"I'll be there," he said. "Sietske, how are your parents? Does Minne's mother know?"

"Yes, she knows. They are all in bad shape." Sietske turned and hurried along the canal. Johannes retraced their footsteps to the farm, flooded with an overwhelming feeling of anger and fear.

Half an hour later he met Sietske at their driveway. She smiled at him, her face still swollen and red.

"I need to be back by four," he said.

"So do I, and if possible, even before. I have to help with the milking now that Klaas and Minne are gone."

"Will you manage?" he asked.

"Yes, we will." A familiar determination shone in her eyes.

They biked in silence for a while, full of their own thoughts. Johannes wondered about Minne. First he'd lost his father, and now he was prisoner. Johannes hoped they wouldn't torture his friend. He hoped they would realize Minne was a boy, even though he'd acted like a grownup.

"You can't tell me why we have to visit this particular bakery?" he asked.

Sietske shook her head. "No, not yet. It is better that you don't mention this place to your parents."

Forty minutes later they entered Leeuwarden. Many people carried firewood on their bikes or in small carts. Military trucks drove past them. Due to the nearby air base and the large prison, more German soldiers were stationed in this provincial capital than anywhere else. Johannes and Sietske pedalled across several bridges. Small and large boats lay along the quay. Houseboats on both sides of the canal were stuck in the ice. Children were having a speed-skating race on one of the canals. An old woman was attempting to cut a hole in the ice with an axe. On the First Canal bridge, they turned right and followed the waterway to the East bridge. The bakery was on the right.

"Let's park our bikes in the alley beside the building," Sietske suggested.

Johannes followed as Sietske opened the door. The jingle of a bell above the door announced their arrival. The smell of freshly baked bread embraced them, and Johannes' stomach growled. The light in the store was dim. They walked up to the counter, then stopped.

Two German soldiers stood talking with a man behind the counter. The man looked up at the two new customers. The two Germans seemed in no hurry to leave the store.

"Can I help you?" the man asked.

Sietske looked at Johannes. It occurred to him that, for the first time, Sietske wasn't quite sure what to say. Clearly, she hadn't expected Germans to be in the store, either.

"I came to buy a loaf of bread," she finally spoke.

The man behind the counter looked from Sietske to Johannes. The two Germans turned around and observed them closely. Johannes shifted awkwardly from one foot to the other.

"I have bread in the oven," the man said. "Come back in an hour."

They both nodded and quickly left the store.

Standing in the alley, Johannes whispered, "What do we do now?"

"We go for a walk," Sietske said. "We'll be back at three. Hopefully, the Germans will be gone by then."

They walked down the same street they'd rode on their bikes. At the corner, they stopped in front of the house where the German Chief Commander Herr Obermann resided. He was in charge of the prison and the House of Detention. Two Nazi soldiers, on either side of the heavy oak door, guarded the house. A large painted sign above the door read: ORTSKOMMANDANTUR [District Commander].

Commander Obermann decided who was to live, who was to die and who needed to be tortured. He was well known for his cruel and sadistic treatment of those who had been caught working against the Nazi regime. The fate of Johannes' friend Minne, Klaas and all the other people who had been captured lay in the hands of this cruel man. Johannes shivered despite his warm clothing.

"Let's go back and walk across the bridge to the prison," Sietske said.

Many children were playing in the street. Women and old men walked in pairs. The Germans had just set a new rule stating that it was forbidden to be in groups of more than two people. Some women carried baskets with laundry.

Over the East bridge, they turned left. The canal in front of the prison was frozen, too. Low-growing bushes leaned against the entrance of the House of Detention. A tall iron gate protected the front door from intruders. High walls hid the house from the outside world. Behind the House of Detention was the actual prison, which was also surrounded by high walls and the canal. House-boats and other vessels were stuck in the canal. In most winters it didn't turn this cold, and the canals stayed open. This year's winter had stopped all transportation along the waterways.

Johannes watched Sietske's pale face as she looked up at the thick concrete wall. He took her hand.

"Where could they be?" she whispered.

Johannes pressed her hand. "My father has told us this much. Political prisoners are all kept in the House of Detention. The regular criminals, those prisoners who had nothing to do with illegal actions against the Germans, are held in the main prison building."

Sietske sighed and they walked along in silence for a while.

"You never told me what happened to the pilot," Johannes said, to change the subject.

"Oh, I'm sorry, Johannes. He was a real English gentleman. I liked the way he spoke, you know, as if he held a hot potato in his mouth. And he was so polite. He told us he came from Liverpool and that he flew a Spitfire to protect the Halifax planes from the German fighters. The pilot slept all night in the shelter. At four o'clock the next morning, Klaas went into the village to get the doctor."

Johannes remembered that the doctor was one of the few people who was allowed to drive a car and be out during curfew.

Sietske continued. "He checked the pilot and diagnosed him as having a concussion and two broken ribs. He gave him a shot of morphine for the pain and we dressed him in women's clothes. The doctor drove him to a safe place. We don't know where he was taken."

"Did the Germans come back?"

"Yes, they came to tell us that the plane had been found, but not the pilot. They asked us to notify them if the pilot showed up," she laughed. "My father said he would."

"You must have a good hiding place," Johannes said.

"Yes, but I can't tell you," she shrugged apologetically.

Johannes smiled. "I won't ask. I'm glad the pilot is safe. They didn't come to search our farm. But of course they would have expected my father to notify them immediately, if we had found the pilot."

They walked in silence for a while. Then, beside a little house, they spotted a clothesline where three articles of clothing — red, white and blue — were hung. Johannes grinned. The colours of the Dutch flag.

"Look." He pointed at the laundry. "It must be the birthday of a member of the royal family. What's the date?"

"I know. It's for the little Princess Margriet, who was born in Canada two years ago." Sietske smiled. "I'm so glad they declared the room she was born in Dutch territory. It would have been awful if our own princess had been born a Canadian. Mother and I forgot to hang our Dutch flag on the clothesline today. We have a red handkerchief, white underwear and a blue sweater on the line every time a member of the royal family celebrates a birthday. The Germans can forbid us to hang out flags, but this we can still do." Johannes heard the satisfaction in her voice.

An artificial bell in the church tower chimed three.

"Let's go back to the bakery," he said.

They walked briskly in the direction of the bake-shop. An army truck stood in front of the gate of the House of Detention. Two soldiers with machine guns guarded the truck. Sietske shivered. They walked faster. No customers were in the store this time.

The man cleaned the counter with a rag. He looked up. His dark eyes observed them closely. "One loaf of bread?" he asked.

Sietske nodded.

"For Sietske?" he added.

"Yes," Sietske answered. "Piet?"

The man nodded. "Here is your bread," he said. He took a loaf of bread from the shelf behind him and wrapped it in parchment paper. "Tonight at seven. Be careful not to lose your bread. It should be cut in the middle."

"Thank you," Sietske said.

"Goodbye," Piet answered.

Sietske opened her coat. Around her neck she wore a burlap bag. She placed the loaf of bread in the bag and closed her coat.

"Just in case they want to check my saddlebags," she said.

Johannes and Piet exchanged nods, then he and Sietske left the bakery. A strong wind slowed the bicyclists down. Neither of them made it home on time.

When Johannes walked into the stable, he avoided his father's questioning stare. Grandfather was still feeding the cows. Johannes quickly grabbed a pail and started on his first cow. Douwe winked at him. Johannes tried to keep his mind on his job, but his thoughts kept wandering to Minne and Klaas. He wondered about the loaf of bread and about the message that must have been hidden inside. Finally, after the last cow was milked and the chores finished, he washed up and went into the kitchen.

His grandparents sat at the table. Anneke poured glasses of milk for everybody. Mother cut the bread. Father came in last.

"Why were you so late this afternoon?" Grandfather started.

"I was at Sietske's." Johannes felt his heart beat faster. He hated his grandfather's questions.

"You can't visit her during the week anymore," Grandfather continued. "There is too much work to be done here. Your father is away a lot."

"They are short-handed, Grandfather. They need my help." Johannes didn't look up from his plate. His cheeks burned.

"Half the Dijkstra family was picked up this morning by the Germans," his father said calmly. Mother gasped and covered her mouth. Anneke jumped off the chair and ran to her father.

"What happened?" she cried.

His father placed one arm around his daughter and looked at Johannes.

"Ask Johannes," he said. "He knows all the details." He gently pushed Anneke away and stood up from the table. "I want to see you in the stable when you've finished explaining," he said. Then he left the kitchen.

# A Time to Choose

All eyes were upon him.

"Please, Johannes, tell us," his mother said.

"This morning Klaas, Minne and six others were captured when they tried to free the provincial leader of the resistance during his transport from Sneek to Leeuwarden."

"Oh, no! Not Minne. Poor Boukje! First her husband, and now her only son." Mother covered her face with her hands.

"They take too many risks," Grandfather spoke. "They have become careless and put too many lives in danger."

Grandmother cried softly. "This terrible war," she sobbed. "How many more lives will be lost before this is all over?"

Anneke placed one arm around her mother's shoulders. "I'll go and see Mrs. de Jong tomorrow," she said. Johannes felt admiration for his little sister.

"We'll go together," Mother said.

Johannes had lost his appetite. He got up from the

table. He looked at his mother. She was calm now, but her eyes flashed with anger. She nodded at him and looked at the door.

Johannes walked into the stable. He found his father sitting on a wooden bench. A small carbide lamp stood on the floor. The windows in the stable had been covered with blackout curtains for the night.

Johannes sat down beside his father. He stared into the light. The cows chewed their cud. The familiar smell of fresh manure and hay filled his nostrils, but didn't comfort him tonight.

"I don't know how much you are involved, Johannes." His father spoke in a tired voice. "And I don't want to know."

Johannes swallowed. His father knew what he was up to? Of course, he wasn't blind. His anger returned. "Minne is my best friend, Father. Klaas is Sietske's brother. If I can do anything to help them, I will."

"No, Johannes. You can't do anything. They're in the House of Detention. They are guarded day and night. There's nothing . . . nothing you or anybody can do."

"What about you, Father? You can do something!" Johannes jumped up from the bench to stand in front of his father.

Slowly his father rose, towering a head above his son. Sadly he looked into Johannes' eyes, as his hands moved up to rest on the boy's shoulders.

"There's nothing I can do either, Johannes. If I tried to free my neighbours, the Nazis wouldn't trust me any longer."

"But Minne, Father — he's only a boy."

"Minne should have thought of that before he got himself into this. He knew what the risks were. And so do you, Johannes. I want you to stay away from Sietske and her family. I don't want you involved!" Father's voice had risen. He leaned heavily on Johannes.

"I'm already involved. I can't stay away from her and I have to do whatever I can to save my friend."

"No! You will not. I forbid you to have anything to do with Sietske!" His eyes looked intently into his son's. Johannes returned the stare. He wasn't willing to give in, not this time. Slowly his father's eyes turned away. His hands slipped off Johannes' shoulders. He slumped back onto the bench. Johannes' hands rolled into fists in his pockets. His bottom lip trembled. He clenched his teeth.

"You made your choice at the beginning of the war, Father. Now the time has come for me to make my choice. I will do anything in my power to help Minne. I'm sorry, but you can't stop me." He sat down on the bench beside his father. Together they watched the tails of the cows in front of them, swishing back and forth, back and forth.

"Next week you will be seventeen, Johannes." Father spoke with difficulty. "I don't know what will happen to me after the war is over, but I want you to be here for your mother and for Anneke."

Startled, Johannes examined his father. He'd lost weight. His cheekbones stuck out and his eyes were sunken. "What will they do to you, Father? They can't do anything, can they? I mean, you haven't betrayed any people, have you?"

"No, I have never betrayed anyone, but there's so much hate against collaborators, Johannes. You never know what other people might do."

"Why don't you give up your membership?" Johannes turned to his father. "You know now what the Germans are up to. You can't ignore how they are exterminating the Jewish people. Even the children. Innocent babies."

"Give it up now? No, Johannes. It's too late. The damage has been done. It wouldn't make any difference now. Do you really think the people here would trust me if I gave up my membership at this stage of the war?" He closed his eyes. The stress of the war showed clearly in the sharp lines etched in his thirty-eight-year-old face.

"Why didn't you resign from the party earlier? Why have you been so damn loyal to those bastards? Have they been blackmailing you?" Johannes stared intently at his father, who was silent. "Why don't you answer my questions?"

His father looked at the ground. "I can't," he said flatly.

Johannes turned. "I'm going to Sietske. Don't try to stop me, Father!"

"Don't expect any help from me when you get into trouble, Johannes. I have no power in the party. I'm only a member."

"I know," Johannes said. "I know not to expect anything from my own father." Grabbing his coat, he opened the stable door and walked into the darkness. He ran across the field, angry tears streaming down his face.

Sietske let him in after three knocks on the window. When he walked into the kitchen, the warmth of the woodstove embraced him. Blue clouds of smoke from homegrown tobacco curled up to the ceiling. Sietske's parents, Bauke and Piet from the bakery were gathered around the table.

Bauke nodded a greeting. "Sit down," he said.

Johannes looked around the table. Sietske's mother slouched in a chair. Deep lines had formed around her eyes and mouth. Mr. Dijkstra's face was the colour of parchment paper. Bauke's face shone with the same determination Johannes was used to seeing in Sietske's. Piet appeared to be in deep thought as he slowly puffed on his pipe.

"We're waiting for Willem," Bauke added.

Johannes squirmed in his chair. He wished the meeting would take place without Willem.

"Here's the key, Piet." Bauke took a key out of his pocket and handed it to the man beside him. "I made one exactly like it. We just have to trust that it fits."

Silence returned to the warm kitchen until at last three loud knocks sounded on the windowpane.

"I'll get it." Bauke answered the door and returned with Willem.

"Evening," he murmured. The people around the table nodded their heads. Just the sight of the man made Johannes edgy.

"Sit down," Sietske's mother said.

Johannes observed the medium-built man as he took his place. Rough and boisterous, he glanced furtively around the table. They stopped at Johannes' face. Johannes felt a hot flash creep up his cheeks. What comment was Willem going to make this time?

"No!" Willem jumped up. His chair scraped back over the wooden floor and hit the dresser with a thud. "No!" He pointed to Johannes. "He is not going to be involved in this operation. I will kill him first."

"Stop!" Bauke said. "You are not the only one here who decides which members take part in what actions." Bauke met Willem's eyes without wavering. Willem didn't back down.

"No? We will see about that. I will remove him from this room myself. Right this minute!"

Perspiration trickled down Johannes' forehead. The muscles in his body tightened. He wasn't going to leave! Certainly not because this pompous man thought he had special privileges. Willem's eyes shifted from Bauke to Johannes. Suddenly he saw Willem take something shiny from his pocket. The blade of a knife flashed in front of Johannes' face.

"Sit down, Willem," said Sietske's father quietly. His calm voice, full of disdain, made Willem turn around. He picked up his chair and sat down again. His eyes never left Johannes' face.

"I don't trust him," Willem snarled. "I'm sure he has told his father about the meeting tonight." He looked around the circle as if asking for support from the others.

"Let's get down to business," Bauke started. "We can't waste any time. My brother and many of our friends' lives are at stake. Piet and I have a plan."

All eyes focussed now on the baker, who sat quietly smoking his pipe as if the incident between Johannes and Willem had never happened.

"The idea came up last night," Piet said slowly. "After Inspector Bakker was arrested by the Germans, I and a few others decided if this morning's operation wasn't successful, we would have to free him from the House of Detention. One of our members, who works as a prison guard, came into the shop this morning. After I told him about the plan, he suggested that the best way to get inside the House of Detention would be through the coal shed. After lunch he gave me the key to that shed."

Johannes' eyes widened. He forgot about Willem. So it had been the key to the coal shed that they had picked up that afternoon hidden in the bread. Bauke had made a duplicate, and that's why he'd returned the key to the baker tonight.

"Can you trust this guard?" Sietske's father asked.

"Yes, Jelle can be trusted. He knows exactly what goes on inside the House of Detention."

"Tomorrow night at eight, we will go in and free the men who were captured this morning and are most at risk of losing their lives. No man can stand the torture the Germans put them through. Eventually even the strongest person will talk and tell the names of the men and women who fight in the resistance. It will be the end for all of us."

A shiver crept up Johannes' spine. How would they get inside the House of Detention unseen? The prisoners were guarded heavily day and night, his father had said.

Sietske was sitting forward on the edge of her chair, listening intently to Piet outline the plan. So many times during the last few months, Johannes had been overwhelmed by her courage and determination. He remembered his pledge to her, that he would give his life to save Minne, Klaas and the others. But now his father's plea haunted him. "I want you to be here for your mother and Anneke," he had said.

"We will go in at eight tomorrow night," Piet said. "Jelle's work shift starts at seven." He looked at their faces. "Inspector Bakker and the people who were picked up this morning must be freed. That's nine prisoners. People, we have only one chance to pull this off. We can't afford to make any mistakes."

Johannes held his breath as Piet continued, "Tomorrow morning I'll get a list of the prisoners' names and their cell numbers. We have six resistance members here tonight. Kees couldn't make it, but he will be with us tomorrow night. I also have two men in town who work for the telephone company, and Jelle, the prison guard. My wife and my mother-in-law will have the names and addresses of hiding places, as well as contact people who will help you hide the prisoners. Willem, I want you to take charge of the firewood for my ovens tomorrow afternoon. Make sure the guns are tied inside the bundles of branches. You know my supplier?"

Willem nodded. "I'll be there and deliver it myself by horse and wagon."

"We'll meet behind the bakery tomorrow night at seven," Piet continued. "Remember, two at a time. You will not be able to make it home after the operation because of curfew." He looked straight at Johannes. "You have to make up an alibi for your family at home."

Johannes nodded. He hoped he could think of something. Perhaps his mother would help. Then he rejected the thought. He didn't want his mother involved this time. She had enough to worry about.

"I count on all of you to be there." Piet's eyes went around the table and rested on every face. "If we're lucky, we won't have to use any force. We'll go in and out in twenty minutes and take the prisoners with us. You'll get your assignment and more details tomorrow night."

Bauke stood up. A lock of curly brown hair covered his forehead. He cleared his throat. "I would like to thank everyone for their commitment." His eyes held Johannes' and moved on to rest on his mother's wary face. "This is very hard for my parents, but I want you to consider what Minne's mother must be going through at this moment as well. And to answer your concerns, Willem, don't you think it is safer to have Johannes with us tomorrow night?"

Willem didn't answer.

Johannes looked up to thank Bauke, but the words didn't come. All he could think of was Minne.

"See you at seven tomorrow night," Bauke said.

"One more thing before you leave. Please bring extra woollen socks to wear over your shoes. We can't make any noise. Remember there are guards in front of Commander Obermann's place," Piet said.

Johannes nodded, stood up and walked to the door. He grabbed his coat and hat in the hallway. Without a word, he left the farm. The cold night air made him gasp. He pulled his scarf tightly over his ears. Clouds had covered the moon.

"Johannes, wait!" Sietske's voice stopped him. He turned around.

She caught up with him and touched his arm. "I'll walk you to the end of the driveway."

He nodded and tucked her arm under his.

"Shall we bike into town together tomorrow night?" she asked.

"What time should I meet you?"

"Let's meet here at six-fifteen," she answered.

"All right," he said. At the road, they stopped. He turned and looked at Sietske. He didn't wonder about Sietske's involvement in dangerous operations anymore. He knew she couldn't stay home and play it safe. With both hands placed on her shoulders, he forced her to look up at him.

"Sietske?"

"Yes," she whispered.

"Do you believe me? Do you trust me?"

She was silent. Slowly her arms wound around his neck. She pulled his head down. Their frost-white breath met.

"Yes, Johannes. I do."

With a relieved sigh, he pulled her closer. They stood there until the moon returned from hiding and the sound of an engine reminded them of curfew.

# A Dangerous Assignment

Johannes folded the piece of paper and left his room. At Anneke's bedroom door he hesitated for a moment. He couldn't make up his mind whether to give Anneke the note or to leave it on his bed. He knocked gently and opened the door. Anneke lay in bed. Her eyes were puffed and red from a bad cold.

"Hi," he said quietly. "I hope you are feeling a bit better."

Anneke nodded and blew her nose in a big red handkerchief. "Will you give this note to Mother when she comes up to say good night?"

"Are you going out now?" his sister asked in a hoarse voice.

"No, not until after milking time, but please don't say anything," he whispered.

"Should I wish you luck in whatever you'll be doing?" she croaked.

Johannes nodded, a lump stuck in his throat.

"I will not be here tonight. When Mother calls me

tomorrow morning, I still won't be back. Will you go down and tell her that I'm sick and won't come down for the milking?"

"Yes, I will. But what do I say when she checks your bed tonight?" Anneke whispered.

"The note says that I have to see a friend in Harlingen and that I won't be back until tomorrow morning after six," Johannes said.

"Will it be dangerous?" Anneke asked.

"No, not really. I must go now." He closed his sister's bedroom door and ran downstairs. In the kitchen, he grabbed a piece of bread and changed into his milking clothes.

When Johannes entered the stable, he stopped dead in his tracks. At the far end, three Germans stood talking to his father. He recognized Herr Obermann. Next to him stood two soldiers. Johannes recovered himself quickly and began his chores.

"*Ah, deine Junge ist schon groß* [Ah, your son is getting big]." Herr Obermann pointed at him.

His father looked at him, but Johannes didn't meet his eyes.

"*Du mußt sofort mit uns nach Harlingen kommen. Wir haben Ärger im Hafen* [You have to come immediately to the city of Harlingen with us. There's trouble at the harbour]," Obermann said to his father.

"*Das ist nicht möglich, die Kühe müssen gemolken werden* [That's not possible, I have to milk the cows]," his father answered.

"*Die Kühe können warten. Du mußt sofort mitkommen* [The cows can wait. You have to come with us right now]."

His father nodded and walked over to the laundry room to change his clothes. As the Germans started leaving the stable, the commander stopped and turned around.

"*Und deine Sohn muß auch mit nach Harlingen kommen* [And your son should also come with us to Harlingen]."

Johannes stood rooted to the spot, with a milking pail in each hand. He looked at his father. Of all nights! This was going to be the most important one in his life. It could even be his last night. And now this damn Nazi had to tell him to come with them. He wouldn't go. They could shoot him first. He looked at his father, his mouth a thin line, his eyes dark with resentment.

*"Nein, meine Sohn muß hier die Arbeit machen* [No, my son has to finish the work here]," his father answered.

The commander looked from Johannes to his father. He nodded, turned on his heels and marched out of the stable, followed by his guards.

From the stable door Johannes watched his father leave. Before climbing into the car, he turned and looked back at Johannes. Could they both be thinking the same thing — that they might not see each other again?

Slowly Johannes exhaled as the car left the property. He walked back to Douwe and handed him one of the two pails.

He settled down beside his first cow. If their action failed tonight, he would either be killed or locked up. His stomach churned. He closed his eyes and leaned against the warm belly of the cow. The wave of nausea passed. He thought about Minne and wondered what physical and mental condition his friend would be in. Had they tortured him?

After finishing his chores, Johannes quietly left the farm and met Sietske at her driveway. Together they biked to Leeuwarden. They barely spoke. The street to the bakery seemed deserted. They went around to the back door. It opened before they had time to park their bicycles.

"You better bring those inside," Piet said. "You won't be needing them again tonight. You realize you can't go home after curfew."

"What time can we leave here tomorrow?" Johannes asked.

"It all depends on how the operation goes tonight," Piet answered.

"Come upstairs," the baker motioned to them. They followed him into a large kitchen-sitting area on the second floor. The room had painted walls in muted colours. The fabric on the furniture was worn and shabby.

Behind the stove stood a woman in her mid thirties. She was the same height as her husband, but much thinner. Her blond hair was tied back in a ponytail. "This is my wife, Jannie," said Piet. "Jannie, here are Sietske and Johannes."

The woman turned to look at them. Her eyes widened. "They are just children. They can't be involved in a risky operation like this! How could you?"

"Sietske's brother and Johannes' friend were picked up yesterday," Piet answered quietly.

"And my youngest brother," Jannie said softly.

"And my son," said a voice near the window. They now noticed an older woman sitting in a chair in front of the window. "The man left before five this afternoon and he hasn't come back," she added, her eyes never leaving the window.

"Who are you talking about, Mother?" Piet said.

"Herr Obermann, the commander," she said.

Johannes walked over to the window. From there he had a view of the entrance to the House of Detention, across the canal. Down the road, he saw the house of Herr Obermann. He cleared his throat. "Herr Obermann has gone to Harlingen, but don't ask me how I know."

Piet nodded. "Hopefully, he'll stay there all night."

One by one, the other members of the resistance climbed the stairs. Sietske's father and Bauke arrived together. Ten minutes later, Willem and a man with bright red hair, named Kees, entered.

"Did I bring you enough firewood for your ovens, Piet?" Willem laughed.

"Yes, that was all right," said Piet. "The guns are in the bedroom. Thanks."

The older woman rolled down a blackout shade to cover the window. Jannie lit a small carbide lamp on the table.

"Now that we're all here," Piet began, "I shall explain the operation." He brushed the hair from his forehead and looked at his wife. She nodded her head slightly.

"Jelle will be inside the House of Detention shortly. His shift starts at seven. I have two men at the telephone company who are going to temporarily disconnect the telephone lines to the House of Detention and Herr Obermann's residence during our operation."

Johannes swallowed. Piet calmly took a folded piece of paper out of his pocket. He opened it and spread it on the table. Everyone gathered around.

"This is a map of the inside of the House of Detention. The administration staff is gone for the night, but two guards usually stay in the office over here. Two others are guarding the prisoners over here." He pointed to a room beside the front door and to the area where the cells were located. "Jelle is one of the guards in the office. He will turn off the alarm in the office at five to eight, after he has tied up his companion."

"What if he fails?" Willem said.

"Then he will pay for it with his life," Piet answered.

Johannes could hear his heart pounding. He glanced at Sietske. Her eyes met his. Would this be the last time he saw her? he wondered. A shiver ran down his spine. Then he thought of Minne and Klaas and all the others locked up, not knowing if they would ever be free again. Sietske winked.

"Hey!" Willem sneered. "You traitor! You'd better pay attention! If something goes wrong tonight, we'll know who's responsible, and you won't live to tell your father!"

With a jolt, Johannes turned. A curse hung on the tip of his tongue, but he swallowed it and straightened his back. His jaw tightened. He wasn't going to give that lowlife any satisfaction. He would prove tonight that he could be trusted. That he wasn't a traitor or a collaborator.

"We have no time to listen to your remarks, Willem," Bauke said tersely.

"Here are the prisoners' cells," Piet continued. He indicated a space behind the front hall. "All the men we will free tonight are locked up on the ground floor. From the side door we will walk through the furnace room and enter the front hall. Double doors separate this hallway from the area where the cells are. The table with the second alarm button is about twenty metres away. Group number one, Bauke and Willem, will overpower the guards and turn off the alarm at the same time." He looked up from the map at the two men facing him. They nodded. "The guards are not all bad, you know. According to Jelle, most guards will put up their hands and cooperate."

Johannes wondered if Piet wasn't painting too rosy a picture.

"Bauke and Willem, you take Inspector Bakker from cell nine and two prisoners, Jan and Ype, from cells twelve and fifteen. Use your weapon only as a very last resort," Piet added. "You," he pointed at Kees, "and myself are group number two. We will free the prisoners in cells six, seventeen and nineteen. Mr. Dijkstra and Johannes will take the prisoners from cells three, two and one, on this side of the hallway." He pointed at the numbers. "You start at cell number one, Johannes."

Johannes nodded. His hands felt damp. Minne, he thought. Minne might be in cell number one.

"All right," Piet said. "This is how we will get from here to the House of Detention. At ten to eight we will cross the canal over the ice, two at a time. Stay close to

*115*

this side of the canal. We don't want the guards in front of Obermann's house to see us. Move to the other side where the coal shed is located, but stay low. Bauke has the key for the shed. I tried it last night. It fits. Remain in the shed until all three groups have made it across the canal safely. We stay there until exactly eight o'clock. Bauke will open the door to the inner courtyard. Cross the courtyard and wait at the side door of the House of Detention. Jelle will open the door and let us in, two at a time. Remember, we can't take any more than twenty minutes for the whole operation." Piet looked around the circle of people.

"Do not use your weapon unless there is no other way! We will gather our prisoners in the front hall and leave the building through the same side door. From the coal shed, we will leave in groups of four and cross the ice at the same spot you arrived. Follow the ice until you're under the East bridge. Jannie has organized a group of women to take over the prisoners. She knows all the hiding places. Jelle and Bauke will need to go into hiding as well." Piet had pulled his wife beside him. "Jannie, Sietske and the other women will take the prisoners to a safe address where they might have to stay for the time being. Except for Bauke and Jelle, you must try to come back to the bakery as soon as possible. I have a hiding space under one of the ovens. Any questions?"

"What . . . " Mr. Dijkstra cleared his throat. "What do we do with the prisoners who are unable to walk?"

"We'll carry them out," Bauke answered. "We don't leave them behind."

"What about the other prisoners?" Jannie asked.

"I know, I know, Jannie." Piet rubbed his head. "I would like to free all of them. But we have to be realistic. The operation already involves a large number of people and hiding places. If we free more people, our chances of success will be much smaller. It is risky enough as it is."

He looked at his watch. "Group one, I want you to go into the bedroom on the left." He pointed to a door. "Pick up your masks and get your Sten gun. Jannie will help you."

Johannes and Sietske's father were next. Jannie handed them a black knitted mask. By the light of the candle, Johannes pulled the socks over his shoes.

"Have you ever used a Sten gun before, Johannes?" Sietske's father gave him the weapon.

"No," he answered. He'd never used any type of gun before.

"Come closer to the light." Mr. Dijkstra motioned. "I'll show you how to use it and how to load it. And put these in your pocket."

Johannes felt the cool metal of bullets in his hand. He stuck them inside his coat pocket. After Sietske's father showed him how to load and fire the gun, they walked back into the main room. He wasn't sure he'd be successful without any practice.

"I'm waiting for a call from our two people at the phone company," Piet said. "In the meantime, we should set our watches."

They all sat down. Quarter to eight, thought Johannes, as he adjusted his watch. Where would he be tomorrow at this time? No, he blotted out the thought. He should concentrate on tonight, on his task. He wouldn't allow himself to make a mistake.

Jannie fumbled with her apron. Her mother wept without a sound. Piet patted his mother-in-law gently on the shoulder. "We have no choice, Mother. If we don't try to get them free, we are all in danger of losing our lives."

The old woman nodded and squeezed his hand.

The sharp ringing of the phone broke the tense silence. The moment had come. Johannes concentrated on controlling his breathing.

"Yes, this is the bakery. Good night."

All eyes were on Piet. "It's time," he said. "Before you leave, you have to remember one more thing. Your password. A woman will approach you and your prisoners under the bridge. She will say 'nine.' Your answer will be 'sharp.' You will leave the prisoners with this person and try to get back to the bakery as soon as possible. Understood?"

They all nodded.

"Bauke and Willem, time to go," Piet ordered.

Bauke hugged Sietske. His eyes met Johannes'. He grabbed his father's hands in both of his. Johannes saw tears in the eye's of the older man, who simply nodded in reply. Then the two men were gone. Piet and Kees followed soon after. Then it was time for Johannes and Sietske's father to say goodbye. She threw her arms around her father. "Be careful. Please bring Klaas back," she whispered.

Her father walked towards the door. Johannes put down the gun and mask and wrapped his arms around Sietske. He couldn't find anything to say to her. Her eyes, round and warm, told him he didn't need to. He kissed her softly on her forehead. He picked up the gun, put on the mask and followed her father outside.

# Inside the House of Detention

With the gun hidden underneath his coat, Johannes followed Sietske's father across the street towards the canal. They were the only people in the street. Darkness had fallen quickly, and it was difficult to see where to get down onto the canal. But once they were on the ice, their sock-covered shoes slid effortlessly across. Cold from the ice penetrated the soles of their shoes. A wooden ladder had been left in place to climb the wall on the other side of the canal. Sietske's father went up first. Johannes stayed close behind him. In silence they walked to the coal shed.

"Are you all right, Johannes?" Sietske's father whispered.

For one moment he thought about his own father. He wished Father were here with them, and on their side. He swallowed twice.

"Yes," he whispered back in a thick voice. Mr. Dijkstra patted him on the shoulder. He opened the door to the coal shed. They could hear the others whispering.

"All right," said Piet. "Johannes and Mr. Dijkstra are

now here. That's all of us."

"Bring your prisoners in here, and we get out the same way as we came in," Bauke said quietly. "Good luck, everybody. Remember, stay calm and don't use your weapons unless you have no other choice."

The air in the small room smelled of coal. It tickled Johannes' nostrils. He pulled the mask over his face.

"Load your guns," said Piet in a low voice. He switched on a small flashlight, throwing enough light to help the men fill the magazines of their guns with bullets.

Bauke and Willem opened the door, left the shed and crossed the inner courtyard. The four other men watched from behind the door. They could see the two shadows moving towards the main building.

"Yes!" Piet whispered. "The side door to the House of Detention is open. Let's go."

Johannes scurried behind the three men, his right hand gripping the gun. Could he kill anyone? he wondered. What would he do if he came eye-to-eye with a German soldier? He'd never even killed a sparrow.

"Here we are," whispered Sietske's father. "You know what to do, Johannes?"

"Yes," he answered.

Piet held the door open. As Johannes walked inside, he could feel a different Johannes taking over. He became calm. Now he knew why he was here: to save his best friend and to prove to Sietske and everybody else that he could be trusted. This was his chance. He wasn't going to fail. He'd rather die. Johannes walked behind the others and quickly closed the door behind him. He squinted in the sudden glare of the bright ceiling lights. He'd forgotten what it was like to have electricity.

Bauke and Willem led the way. In the hallway, the lights were dimmer. On the walls their shadows loomed ahead of them. They turned left and stopped in front of a heavy steel door. Behind this door were the cells, Johannes remembered from the map. Cell number one was on the right side at the far end.

The small group of men stood still. They were joined by a man in uniform — Jelle. "I'll open the door, so they'll see me first," he whispered. "Then, you can surprise them. Before I let you in I checked on them. They were both at the table, playing cards. If we're lucky, they're still there. I don't think they'll put up a fight. Remember, the alarm button is on the left side, on the table. We'll be right behind you. And don't shoot unless I tell you."

"Do you have the keys to the cells?" Piet whispered.

Jelle nodded and patted the bulk in his pocket.

"Ready," Jelle mouthed. All heads ducked down. As Jelle pushed open the heavy door, Johannes felt the moisture trickle down his spine. Bauke and Willem ran ahead.

A guard shouted, "Hey! What do you think you're doing?" They both grabbed for their revolvers, but the two resistance members were faster. The guards dropped their guns and raised their arms. Bauke yanked the alarm off the table and cut the wire.

"Kees, keep your gun aimed at these two men while I open the cells."

By now, the prisoners had realized that something was going on. Someone began to yell, "Let me out of here! Whoever you are, let me out!"

Piet called out the numbers and Jelle began to open the doors.

"Hey, you missed my door," a man shouted.

"Sorry," Piet said. "We can't take everybody, but don't give up. The war is almost over."

"Lock the guards in cell number nine as soon as Inspector Bakker is out," Bauke called.

"Kees, get the guard from the administration office in here. He can join the other two," Jelle added.

Johannes ran to the far end to cell number one. "Minne?" he whispered. He heard someone moan. "Minne," he called again.

Across from him, he heard the jangling of keys. A door opened and a voice cried out, "You stupid idiots, what are you trying to do? Get everyone killed?"

"Shut up and be quiet. Do exactly as I tell you." Johannes recognized the gruff voice of Willem.

There were more cries and scuffling sounds. Johannes counted the seconds. When was Jelle coming to open Minne's cell? He felt a cramp in his right arm and realized it was from gripping the gun with all his might. His face felt hot under the black mask.

Beside him, in cell number two, Sietske's father was reunited with Klaas. He could hear the anguish in Mr. Dijkstra's voice.

Finally, Jelle came to open Minne's cell door. "Take him to the front hall," he said.

Johannes pushed the door open. In the small dark space, with only a bed and a pail for comfort, stood Minne. His sweater was ripped; bloodstains covered the front. A white bandage was wrapped around his head.

"Minne!" Johannes cried. "What have they done to you?" Gently, he touched his arm. "Come! Come away from this damn place."

Minne threw his arms around his friend. "Oh, Johannes, get me out! This is hell! The next time the bastard gets his hands on me I won't be able to stay silent. I'm sorry, I can't take it anymore." His sobs broke unevenly. Johannes felt the body in his arms tremble.

"You don't have to take it any longer. Come now. Quickly!"

Johannes felt the tears well in his eyes as he helped his friend walk out of the cell and down the hall, the other prisoners stumbling ahead of him. Nothing must happen now. The prisoners were so close to freedom.

Just a few more minutes. He pulled his mask down over his face.

The prisoners and their rescuers were standing in the front hall. A tall, middle-aged man with two swollen eyes, a cut lip and two bandaged hands leaned against Piet — Inspector Bakker, Johannes thought. They had really worked him over. The man could hardly walk. Johannes also recognized Jan, another prisoner from the raid on the local distribution office in December. He didn't know any of the other men except Klaas.

"Listen, everybody," Piet said. "So far so good. We just need a few more minutes to leave through the side door and wait in the coal shed. Someone will tell us when the coast is clear. Make no sound. Try to get under the bridge as fast as possible. If you see trouble, you must go to the first houseboat. Use your password!"

Inspector Bakker raised his head. "I want to thank . . . "

A-A-A-N-N-N!

The front bell. Johannes thought his heart had stopped beating. He held onto Minne, who started moving away from him.

"Stop," Piet whispered. "Move all the prisoners back to cell seventeen. Don't make a sound."

The bell rang for the second time. Kees pushed the group back through the heavy door into the cell area.

"Turn on the outside light, Jelle," Piet ordered. "Everybody have your gun ready and move into the director's office, but leave the door ajar so you can hear what's going on. Don't use your guns unless I give the order. Jelle, open the door and let them in."

Johannes ran quickly with the other men into the director's office. They heard Jelle open the door. From where he stood, Johannes could see the front entrance.

"Who is it?" Jelle commanded in a loud voice.

"We have a prisoner, but we couldn't notify you. Something is wrong with the phone," a man's voice answered.

"There's trouble with the phone line," Jelle replied. "Someone's fixing it now. Come in." He opened the door further. A huge man and a German Security Officer dragged their prisoner inside. The man had been roughed up already.

"That's him," Sietske's father said in a low voice. He grabbed his gun.

"No, Father!" Bauke whispered. "Don't!"

"It's Johanson! The German brute! The animal! The dirty Nazi who beat me up while they held me here."

The one who'd tortured Minne, too, and all the other political prisoners, Johannes guessed. Bauke held on to his father. The normally calm farmer was close to losing his self-control. Sweat poured down Johannes' face. They were not going to get out alive now, he felt it. Everything was going wrong. They would all be executed after they'd been in the unmerciful hands of this monster.

"I need some help!" Jelle called.

"Don't use your weapon," Bauke ordered. "Overpower the officer and Johanson! No bloodshed!"

He pushed the door open and the six men dashed into the hall. Bauke jumped the officer, who didn't put up a fight. Instead, he dropped his revolver and raised his hands. Willem ran straight for the brute Johanson. The Nazi crashed to the floor. Willem fell on top of him before he could reach for his weapon. They tumbled across the hall floor. Johanson, who had the strength of a body builder, didn't give up easily.

The two struggling men were soon bleeding from cuts on their faces. But Willem finally got the beast under control. While Willem held him down, Kees reached inside Johanson's pockets and pulled out a revolver and two knives.

"We're losing too much time," Mr. Dijkstra said evenly. He pointed his gun at Johanson.

"No!" Bauke restrained his father. "If we kill one German, ten prisoners will be executed in retaliation, remember?"

"All right, put the handcuffs on and let's lock him up." Jelle grabbed Johanson's hands and closed the cuffs on him. They yanked him off the floor. Johannes looked into hate-filled eyes staring out of a bloodied face. He shivered. He could better understand Minne's plea. Anger surged through his body, and for the first time, he felt he could kill another being. This animal had brutalized his friend. For the rest of his life he would remember that face.

Kees and Bauke locked up the policeman and a swearing Johanson in cell number one.

"Quick, get the prisoners out!" Piet commanded. They ran back to cell seventeen to get their charges, then headed for the door.

Almost forgotten, the new prisoner stood beside the front door, leaning against the post. The man's bottom lip was swollen and split open. His hands were cuffed behind his back. Blood trickled down his chin.

"Who are you? Why did they bring you here?" Bauke asked.

"I'm Doctor Wartens," he said hoarsely. "The Germans didn't like the way I treated the prisoners. They picked me up this afternoon and Johanson had some fun with me before they brought me here."

"We'll take you with us and find you a hiding place," Bauke said. Johannes saw tears welling up in the doctor's eyes. He looked like he wanted to say something, but he wasn't able to. Jelle took the keys and freed him from the handcuffs. The doctor staggered forward and grabbed Bauke's hand.

"Thank you. Thank you. All of you." He covered his face with his hands. Johannes swallowed.

"Johannes, Minne, Klaas, Dijkstra — back through the side door into the coal shed!" Piet ordered. "Jelle, take the doctor. Everybody move! Now!"

As they opened the side door, the phone in the administration office started ringing.

"The interruption in the phone line has been repaired," Piet said. "That means our time is up. Let's get out of here!"

The group stumbled across the courtyard to the shed.

# A Long Night

In the small coal shed, the rescuers and the rescued were jammed together. It was difficult for the injured ones to get any relief from their pain.

"We have to wait for our contact person," Piet whispered. "She should have been here by now."

Within seconds someone tapped three times on the door. Piet opened the door a little and a familiar voice whispered, "Herr Obermann has returned, so be careful. Move as quietly and quickly as possible. The ladder is in the same spot as when you came in."

Johannes' hands balled into fists. Why did Sietske do all the dangerous work?

"Move!" Piet ordered.

One by one the prisoners and their rescuers moved out of the coal shed. Johannes lowered himself onto the ladder to support Minne, who had difficulty moving his feet from one rung to the next. He complained about being dizzy — a concussion, Johannes thought. Carefully he covered Minne's head with his toque to conceal the white bandage. Klaas and his father followed. Klaas limped badly. That bastard Johanson had had his fun with Klaas, too. A bitter taste surged into Johannes' mouth.

Johannes gently pushed Minne's head down as they slid across the ice to the other side of the canal. Much slower than they had anticipated, the group moved to the East bridge. All the time, their eyes never left the House of Detention. By now, someone from the Obermann residence must have noticed that something was wrong at the prison.

"You two go ahead of us," Mr. Dijkstra said.

"Lean on me, Minne," Johannes urged.

"Not so fast," came Minne's weak plea.

Johannes gripped his friend under the elbow. He wished he could get rid of the gun. "We have to, Minne. You can't give up now." Minne didn't answer.

After what seemed a much-too-long journey, Johannes and Minne arrived under the bridge. Some of the others were there, hunched close together. Already their group had dwindled. Some had already been taken to their hiding places.

"Is Minne all right?" Johannes recognized Piet's voice.

"I think he might have a concussion," Johannes answered in a lowered voice. His eyes scanned the group for Sietske, but he didn't see her. Piet moved beside him.

"Listen, Johannes. You think you can manage to get him to the first houseboat?"

"Yes," Johannes said. "If I can get rid of the gun, I'll carry him."

"You might need it later on. You never know," Piet whispered.

"I can't hold both Minne and the gun. I have no choice."

"Give me the gun," Piet said.

Johannes handed the gun over. Bending over, he took the weight of his friend across his shoulders. He stood up. Minne had lost consciousness. He felt as heavy as lead.

"Good work, Johannes. And good luck!" Piet patted him on the back.

A car engine revved at the same moment as Johannes carried his load out from under the bridge.

"Wait!" Piet said. They heard the sound of a car door being slammed. The car surged forward, tires screeching, and made a left turn across the East bridge. It halted in front of the gate to the House of Detention. "Now! Everybody hide behind the first houseboat, then move on!"

Johannes staggered under the weight of his friend. He couldn't keep up with the others. He stayed close to the canal wall. He heard doors slam. Expecting searchlights on him at any time, he moved on, sweat pouring down his face and body. He couldn't take the mask off.

At last he felt a rope, and groped with one hand for the side of the houseboat. When his hand touched glass, he knocked three times. He was alone. The rest of the group must have moved on ahead.

The sound of a door opening was followed by soft footsteps. The shadow of a person came closer. Johannes waited until the person reached him. His heavy load began to slip off his shoulders.

"Nine," a woman's voice said.

"Sharp," Johannes answered.

"I'll help both of you inside. We'd better hurry. By now they have discovered what has happened."

With the woman's help, Johannes carried Minne around to the houseboat's entrance. He stumbled several times in the dark, but they made it. Before going inside, they heard the car turn and roar across the bridge. Then it came to a halt. The car had reached the house of Herr Obermann, Johannes guessed. Now the action would begin.

"Mother, get the shelter ready. Quickly." An older woman, who had been sitting at a table in the tiny kitchen, leapt up and pushed the table aside. She then rolled up the rug and lifted a door that led below. The opening was narrow, but Johannes managed to carry his friend down the five steps.

The young woman followed. With her flashlight, she motioned him to a bed in the corner. Johannes had to stoop to keep from bumping his head on the low ceiling. Slowly he lowered his cargo onto the bed. Then he sat down beside Minne. He took his mask off and looked at the woman. She was of medium height with blond, curly hair. Her eyes looked warily from Johannes to Minne.

He began. "My name is . . . "

"No, no," she said. "We should not introduce ourselves. It's better not to know names."

Johannes nodded. "Thank you for hiding us. You are risk . . . "

"Shh." She put her finger to her lips. "Listen! Army trucks! Two . . . three . . . four! They will be coming soon. I must go upstairs. Keep your friend quiet!" Then she climbed the stairs and closed the door, leaving them in the pitch-black room.

Johannes listened to Minne's breathing. "Minne," he whispered. There was no answer.

He felt around with his hands. Maybe he could find a blanket to cover Minne and keep him warm. Through the thin walls of the boat, he could hear the pounding of boots. German soldiers! His heart jumped as the boots came nearer. The boat trembled under the weight of the soldiers.

"*Aufmachen* [Open the door!]"

Loud bangs on the door and the harsh voice of a Nazi soldier sent ice down Johannes' spine. He felt grateful Minne was unconscious. Above him, he heard footsteps walking towards the door. The door opened. Soldiers marched inside the houseboat. Johannes sat frozen on the bed beside Minne, his hand on his friend's arm.

"*Wir müssen das Boot durch suchen. Heute abend sind zehn Gefangene entflohen* [We have to search the boat. Tonight ten prisoners have escaped]."

Johannes thought his heart had stopped. He was sure the Nazis would find them. He heard the soldiers walking above his head, moving furniture back and forth. Opening doors. Dumping drawers and their contents onto the floor. Johannes stared at the spot where he knew the door was.

He waited for it to open. Silence. The seconds ticked away. Then the boots marched to the door. The boat shifted slightly against the ice as the soldiers climbed back onto the quay.

Slowly Johannes released his breath. He heard more running boots and German commands shouted down the street. He wondered how many would be as lucky as he and Minne had been. He stretched his aching arms and legs. He touched Minne's face. It felt cold, but he was still breathing.

A chair scraped across the floor above. A few minutes later the door opened, and the young woman came down with a blanket. "I want you to leave," she said.

"But the streets are full of German soldiers!" Johannes protested.

"I'll get you some women's clothes. Walk along the ice to the last houseboat. From that point, climb onto the quay and disappear behind the row of houses on your left. You can cross the bridge there. Hide behind the houses until you find yourself behind the bakery. You can't stay here any longer." She spread the blanket over Minne. "Someone will come for your friend soon."

"He needs medical treatment," Johannes said.

"I know," she answered. "As soon as we are able, he will get treatment. For now he needs to be safe. And this boat is not a good place." She handed Johannes a bundle of clothes. "Here, I'll leave the flashlight with you. Put the skirt on and tie the scarf around your head. When you're finished, bring the flashlight upstairs with you."

Johannes pulled the skirt over his pants. He had more difficulty tying the scarf around his head. Before he left, he patted Minne's hand.

"I'll see you after the war is over," he whispered. "Don't give up." Minne didn't respond.

With a heavy heart, Johannes climbed the stairs and closed the door behind him. The young woman smiled at him and adjusted his scarf. It occurred to him that he must look funny.

"Take care," she said, as she let him out the door.

He climbed down onto the ice and almost tripped over his skirt. He pulled it up and held on to it while he scampered from boat to boat. From behind one of the boats, he could see the outside lights of the House of Detention. They were probably checking every house and boat in the area. How was he going to find his way to the bakery behind the houses when he couldn't see a thing?

Johannes slid behind the last houseboat. A dog started barking inside. He found his way to the concrete stairs leading onto the quay. He stayed low and peered up and down the street. Then, as fast as he could, he ran across the road and behind the first house. He followed a small alley that led between the row of buildings.

Many times he stopped and listened. German soldiers were sure to be all over this part of the city. Some used dogs to find fugitives. It felt like forever before he finally reached the bridge. Crossing the street, the bridge and then the next street in one run could be dangerous. The road in front of him seemed deserted.

Keeping low, he moved to the bridge. He dropped to his knees to observe the area and to catch his breath. He could see lights on the East bridge. The Germans had blocked the road. Nobody could get close to the House of Detention. He wondered if it was wise to return to the bakery. He wouldn't want to jeopardize anyone's life.

He crawled across the bridge on his hands and knees. In the distance, he heard a church bell chime ten times. Two whole hours had passed since they'd started their mission at the House of Detention.

Checking both ways, he slipped through the streets until he arrived behind the first houses on East Canal Street. His heart pounded in his chest as he crept closer to the bakery — closer to the enemy.

Behind the bakery lay several barrels, planks and crates. Johannes moved carefully to avoid making a noise. He reached the back door and stopped. With his ear to the door, he listened. Everything was quiet. All he could hear were orders being shouted to soldiers in front of the bakery. Had Piet and his family been picked up by the Germans? Had the Nazis found out who was responsible for the escape?

A door opened and closed inside the bakery. Johannes slowly turned the handle of the back door. It squeaked as he opened it.

"Who's there?" a voice asked.

Johannes recognized Piet's voice. He exhaled. "It's me, Johannes," he whispered.

"Quickly. Come inside." Piet reached for him and pulled him into the darkness of the bakery. He could feel the welcome heat from the oven. Piet moved aside a large box filled with twigs and eased open a door in the wooden floor.

"Get down and don't make a sound until I come to get you."

"Who else is down there?" Johannes asked. Was Sietske there, safe? he wondered.

"Sietske's father and Kees," Piet answered. "The others are in hiding."

"And Sietske?" Johannes asked.

"Go down there now," ordered Piet. "Sietske might come by later."

Sietske might come by later, Johannes thought as he descended the stairs. Piet made it sound like an ordinary visit. So Sietske was lost, wandering in the city by herself. A city full of German soldiers. He stopped and turned.

"I'm going back," he said. "I'll look for her!"

"No, Johannes." Piet pushed his head down. "Nobody is going to look for her. Not her father, not Kees, not me and not you. Move!" He shoved Johannes down the steps. He had to steady himself by placing his hands on the wall.

The door closed above him. Defeated, Johannes felt his way down the stairs. A small candle sitting on a crate threw a dim light. In the corner, he saw two men sitting on the floor.

"Come join us, Johannes," Kees spoke. "All we can do now is wait and hope for the best."

"Did all the prisoners get to their hiding places in time?" Johannes asked.

"We don't know," said Mr. Dijkstra. "We don't know how safe their hiding places are right now."

Johannes pulled off his scarf and skirt and sat down on the floor, his back against the wall. He thought about the action of the last few hours. It all seemed like a bad dream. He began to shake as the events passed through his mind. He covered his head with his hands. Neither of the other two men spoke. His thoughts returned to Sietske. Had he lost her forever?

At last he dozed off. Some time later they heard a movement above them. Johannes lifted his head. The candle had burnt itself out. He couldn't tell if the other two were asleep or not. Footsteps crossed the floor, followed by the squeaking of the back door.

Was it Sietske? He held his breath and listened. The footsteps came nearer. The box with firewood was dragged aside, and the door above the stairs opened.

His heart skipped a beat when he saw her coming down the stairs supported by Piet, who was holding a flashlight. She was limping. In seconds, her father was at her side. He put his arm around her shoulders. Her face had turned a greyish-white colour. Tears rolled down her cheeks.

"I'm all right," she sobbed. "I got everybody to their hiding places. I was so worried about you and Johannes getting back to the bakery. I had to wait and hide in an old shed for a long time. The soldiers were everywhere. I thought they would discover me when they came around behind the houses with their dogs. I was so lucky." She shook in her father's arms. Johannes felt an overwhelming urge to hold her close and protect her from the rest of the world. But he kept his feelings to himself.

Curfew lifted at six in the morning. Piet came down to tell Johannes to put his female clothes back on, get his bike and head out the back door. Johannes dressed quickly. He took one last look at Sietske. She was sound asleep in her father's arms. A little colour had returned to her cheeks.

"Will you have trouble getting home?" Piet asked when Johannes was ready to leave.

"No, it's still dark out. I'm sure I can get into the house and in my bed without anybody knowing."

"Avoid the main roads. The Germans might have set up checkpoints," Piet said. "Take care. And thank you, Johannes."

# Evacuees

"I can't believe it! What a stunt!" Grandfather's voice boomed through the kitchen.

Johannes waited before he opened the door into the room. They believed he was sick, so when he sat at the table he would have to eat as little as possible. Johannes grimaced. He was starving.

It seemed that everything had worked out in his favour that morning. The night before, Anneke had told Mother about his visit to Harlingen. And when his mother had called him at five in the morning, Anneke had gone downstairs and explained that he wasn't feeling well, that he was too sick to milk the cows. Later, Johannes had slipped inside unseen.

After breakfast his mother had brought him a glass of milk. All she had said was, "I don't believe you went to Harlingen to help a friend. I worried all night, Johannes. I hope what you put me through was worth it. I'm glad you're safe in your bed. Go to sleep now." She'd stroked the hair back from his face. Johannes hadn't even heard her leave.

Now he rested his head against the wall.

"A masterpiece!" his grandfather went on. "It's unbelievable. They went in, took ten prisoners, locked up all the guards and didn't shed a single drop of blood! It's incredible. These people deserve a medal!"

Johannes entered the kitchen. The family was sitting around the table, ready for the evening meal.

"How are you feeling, Johannes?" Grandmother looked at him, concern in her eyes.

"Much better," he answered, not looking at her. "I slept most of the day." That much was true. He *had* slept most of the day.

"Did you hear what happened?" Grandfather started all over again.

Johannes didn't answer.

"Members of the resistance walked into the House of Detention last night and liberated ten political prisoners, one of them Inspector Bakker, the leader of the provincial organization. They didn't use any force and not a single drop of blood was spilled. I can't get over it!"

Johannes nodded.

"I hope they found Minne," his mother said.

Johannes buttered his bread. He didn't look at his mother. He wished he could tell her, but he would jeopardize his family's safety if they knew of his involvement.

"Did you hear of any names besides Inspector Bakker's?" Mother asked. Grandfather shook his head.

"Why don't you find out, Durk?"

Father remained silent. He was watching his son eat his bread.

Johannes felt his face grow hot. He looked up from his plate to meet his father's gaze. Was it his imagination, or did he see his father's eyes gleam? Was it pride? Did his father know where he had been last night? He sighed and tried to swallow his bread. He didn't dare ask.

"I wonder what the retaliations will be?" His mother

broke the silence. They all wondered, but no one voiced an opinion.

In the next few days nothing happened. Wanted posters with the names of the ten political prisoners went up in every town and city. When she found out that Minne and Klaas were among those in hiding, Johannes' mother danced around the table with Anneke. She often looked at Johannes, but she didn't ask.

To everybody's surprise, there were no retaliations. Herr Obermann wanted to organize a large manhunt and search the whole town of Leeuwarden, but he needed the assistance of the commander of the air base. And the commander had refused. Rumour had it he thought the whole operation was a masterpiece.

Times were tough at Sietske's farm. With Bauke, Klaas and Minne in hiding, they were short-handed. Once in a while, Johannes helped out, but he was needed too much at home.

Sietske still seemed shaken by the events. She had lost weight and was often silent. She worked day and night and did most of the chores her brothers would normally have done. Her grandparents had moved in. They did the housekeeping so Mrs. Dijkstra could be free to do farm work.

In February, a black car drove into the van der Meer driveway. Two men in suits climbed out. His mother answered the front door. Johannes left the door to the hallway open so he could hear the conversation.

"You are Mrs. van der Meer?" Johannes heard the deep voice of one of the men. They were not German.

"Yes, what can I do for you?" his mother answered politely.

"We are members of the committee for evacuees. Due to heavy fighting in the southern parts of the country, the Germans have evacuated the people from this area. In the next few days we expect a train full of evacuees, and we have assigned you a family with three boys."

"Oh," was all he heard his mother say.

"These people have lost everything, their homes and their livelihoods. That area has become the combat zone of the Allied troops. Whole families have been put on trains by the German soldiers. Here are the names of the family members who will stay with you."

"When will they be here?" his mother asked.

"Thursday or Friday," the man answered. Johannes heard the men bid his mother goodbye. She quietly closed the door. Back in the kitchen she sat down at the table, her face in her hands.

"Three boys and their parents. Oh, those poor people," she said. "Just imagine to have lost everything. I think we should be grateful we still have so much . . . and each other." Tears ran down her face. She brushed them away with her apron and stood up.

"We better get to work. Johannes, you and Anneke will have to share the same room. It's better if you move in with Anneke. Your room is big enough for the three boys."

"What about their parents?" Johannes asked.

"We'll make a bedroom in the laundry room. Grandfather and Grandmother can't go home yet. They have no fuel for their stove." Johannes made a face. "Don't look at me like that, Johannes," she smiled. "We will be a bit crowded, but we will manage. Come on. You start clearing away things in the laundry room." She poked him between the ribs.

A *bit* crowded, he thought. It was going to be like a madhouse with so many people. He hoped the three boys would be old enough to help out; then he could give Sietske's family a hand. Grandfather could boss them around instead of him.

Cold and hungry, the evacuees arrived in Leeuwarden that Friday morning. They were piled onto open wagons like cattle. A young couple with three little boys were dropped off at the van der Meer farm. The boys were eight, four and six months old. Johannes and his mother had cleared the laundry room behind the kitchen and improvised a double bed. A crib was retrieved from the attic and cleaned for the baby. The two older boys were given Johannes' room.

Johannes' mother and grandmother had cooked a big pot of soup. The new family sat quietly at the table. With fear-stricken eyes set wide in their thin, white faces, the two boys watched Anneke and Johannes closely.

"We were loaded onto the trains like animals," the man spoke. "The trains drove through Germany close to the Dutch border. The Germans were afraid of Allied bomb attacks. We stopped often to let more people on. We weren't allowed to leave the train to buy food. At every station I would sneak out to scoop up some snow in my cap, so we had something to drink. We never got any food and the wagons were not heated. We thank you for taking us in," he added, looking at Johannes' mother. The baby cried and the young mother looked around helplessly.

"I don't have enough to feed him," she said in a low voice.

"Anneke, get me some milk," Mother ordered. "We'll heat some for the baby, but first you have to eat the soup and warm yourself in front of the stove."

In the next few days, Sjakie and Sjors, the two older boys, became accustomed to Johannes' family. Johannes took them to see the calves. They told him that they used to have calves at home.

"And a hundred cows," Sjakie, the oldest, told Johannes.

"Not quite," said Sjakie's father, who was standing by. Johannes laughed.

The man, Pierre, was a good worker, but now Johannes

and Anneke were often stuck watching the two eldest boys. Grandmother found the boys too noisy when they were in the house, so they were often sent to the stable. The baby grew stronger by the day, but still cried a lot. The young woman, Maria, didn't say much. She was still too weak to do any work. Johannes' intentions of helping out Sietske's family never materialized.

The end of the war was coming closer. The Germans, who were running scared, managed to find and kill many 'divers' during their manhunts in those last weeks. The resistance was now busy blowing up bridges and railroads, as well as putting up road blocks to prevent the Germans from fleeing back to Germany. Heavy fighting occurred in many towns and villages. Many people lost their lives — soldiers from the Dutch Interior Army, the *NBS* . . . and innocent civilians.

# Liberation

"The Canadians are here! The Canadians are here!" Johannes heard a familiar voice outside. It was the morning of April 15. He dropped his pitchfork and ran out of the stable. Sietske threw her arms around his neck, almost knocking him over.

"What are you talking about? Which Canadians are here?" he laughed as he pulled her into his embrace.

"The Canadian troops are moving in from the northeast. Father says it's only a matter of hours before we are liberated, Johannes." She kissed him on his lips and curled her arms tightly around his neck. "I can't believe it, Johannes. Finally, after five years, we are going to be free."

Johannes looked into her eyes. The sparkle he had missed since the operation in the House of Detention had returned. Her cheeks were flushed.

"And they'll all be home," she sang.

"All right, I'd like some more information," Johannes laughed. He pulled her down to sit beside him on a bench next to the stable. The smell of spring embraced them. Fresh green grass had pushed its new shoots through the dark soil.

Laughing with excitement, she told him of the BBC announcement. The Allied troops were making good progress in the north. Three weeks before, on March 24, General Montgomery's troops had crossed the Rhine at Wezel, a German town about thirty kilometres east of the Dutch border. The First Canadian Army under General Harry D.G. Crerar moved north to cut off the Germans and to liberate the Groningen-Friesian coastal line. The Germans didn't pose much resistance.

"And by today they expected the Canadian troops to move into Leeuwarden," she added. "Isn't this wonderful?"

"Yes." Johannes could hardly believe it. Finally, this damned war was coming to an end. Now everybody would go home and they could be a family again. Just the four of them. And Minne would be back. Perhaps they could do things together as they used to do.

"I hope Klaas, Bauke and Minne come home soon," Sietske said. "I'd better go. There is so much to do. And when I've finished, I'll have time to spend with you."

"Wonderful," he grinned.

Sietske kissed him quickly, turned and ran down the driveway.

Grandfather poked his head around the stable door. "What was all the excitement about?"

"The BBC said the Canadian troops should reach Leeuwarden today."

"It's about time," Grandfather growled as he moved back into the stable.

At noon, as the family ate their meal, they could see German soldiers running down the road in the direction of Harlingen.

"Good, let them be scared for once," Grandfather said. "They can run them all into the Waddensea."

Johannes' father didn't look up from his food. He hadn't said much in the last couple of days. Often, he'd been out with Herr Obermann. Johannes had a growing sense of fear. What would happen to his father now that the Germans had lost?

"Oh, no!" Mother looked out the window. "There's a group of soldiers running up the driveway. You talk to them, Durk!"

Slowly his father stood up and walked into the hallway to the front door.

"*Aufmachen* [Open the door]!" they shouted.

Everybody around the table stopped eating. Grandmother's hand trembled and her spoon dropped into the soup. They heard boots stomping into the hallway. The kitchen door opened.

"They want food," Father said.

Mother stood up. Her jaw tensed. "Tell them they can have food," she said firmly, "but they have to take off their boots and leave their rifles in the hallway."

A moment later, five Germans stumbled into the kitchen without rifles or boots. The family stood up and backed away from the table. The soldiers sat down. Mother fetched some more bread, homemade butter and cheese.

The men looked like they hadn't eaten for days, and they were unshaven. Johannes saw an expression of disgust cross his sister's face. They smelled, he realized.

The Germans gobbled down their food. One soldier seized a piece of bread and stuffed it inside his uniform. After they'd finished their meal, they hurried to leave. Shoving their feet into their boots and grabbing their weapons, they stumbled out of the house. One soldier took the time to say thank you.

"Meek as lambs," Grandfather commented.

"I'll make some more food for us later," Mother said. "Let's clear the table for now. I hope we don't get more of those visitors."

Johannes went into the stable, followed by Sjakie and Sjors.

"Johannes, can we play in the hayloft?" Sjakie asked.

So much for peace and quiet, he thought. "Yes, but you can't go near the bull's stable. Remember, he loves to eat little boys."

"Yes, we know," the boys answered in unison.

Johannes tried to concentrate on feeding the cows, but his thoughts kept returning to his father. What would happen to him?

"Johannes, Sjakie, Sjors!" Anneke shouted. "Come outside! There are tanks on the road. Come and see!"

Johannes grabbed the boys and they ran with Anneke to the end of the driveway. Mother, Grandfather, Grandmother, Maria with the baby and Pierre were all ahead of them. There was no sign of his father. Johannes looked back at the farm, but didn't see him.

Then he saw the tanks and jeeps, all carrying the Canadian flag. Singing and crying, a crowd of people was running and dancing behind the tanks. A few young boys were perched on top of the tanks with the soldiers.

The soldiers waved. Johannes and all the others waved back. "Thank you!" his mother shouted, tears running down her face. He swallowed hard, his eyes misting over.

A Canadian soldier stood up on one of the tanks and yelled in English, "You are FREE, people! You are FREE!"

It was so much like watching a parade or seeing a movie that Johannes wasn't sure it was really happening. They just stood there and waved and cried. The Canadians threw chocolate bars, cigarettes and gum at them. Sjakie and Sjors danced around their father.

"I want to go on one of those." Sjakie pointed at the army tanks.

"Me, too," Sjors cried. "When I grow up, I'll become a soldier and ride on a tank and kill Hitler!"

"Let's hope that won't be necessary," Pierre said. "There will be no more wars!" He kissed Maria's wet cheek and took the baby from her arms. "And in a few days we can go home," he added.

Later in the afternoon, when it was time to milk the cows, everyone settled down a little. Douwe walked into the stable singing the Dutch national anthem. The cows turned their heads and stared at him.

"We can take down the blackout curtains," Pierre suggested. "The nights will be quiet without the air raids. I wonder if we will be able to sleep without the sound of sirens and the droning of planes."

Johannes watched his father do his chores. He worked quietly, but there was a tension in his body that Johannes could sense every time he walked by.

Finally, Johannes moved to his last cow. He would certainly go to visit Sietske tonight, and perhaps they could bike into the village. They didn't have to worry about curfew. Softly he patted the cow on the stomach.

Then there was a sudden commotion at the door.

Three, four, then five men stormed inside. They wore black toques and masks, and black bands were tied around their upper right arms. Johannes felt his heart lurch.

"Freeze everyone!" shouted one man, the tallest of the group. He waved his gun in the air. All five carried weapons that were now all too familiar to Johannes. The tall one seemed to be the leader. He wore another armband with the letters DOL — District Operation Leader — emblazoned on it. Suddenly, Johannes knew who they were. People called them the Black Partisans or Bolsheviks, but he didn't really know what it meant.

The leader moved in between the two rows of cows. "Anybody who runs will get killed!" His speech was slurred. The other four laughed loudly, as if it was a good joke.

"Who is Durk van der Meer?" the tall man commanded.

"I am," his father answered quietly.

Johannes looked over at his father. Their eyes met. Father's seemed to say, "I made my choice, now I will take the consequences."

"You come with us. Now!" the leader ordered.

Fear gripped Johannes' chest as he watched his father walk towards the men. One of them grabbed and quickly handcuffed his father. The stable door opened and the men, laughing, pushed his father outside.

The last man turned back. "We'll make sure these traitors get what they deserve," he chuckled.

Johannes swallowed. Did he know that laugh? Even though it sounded muffled by the woollen mask, did he recognize that laugh?

Then a sudden thought sent a cold chill down his spine.

Willem?

# The Ordeal

Johannes, Douwe and Pierre stood in shocked silence. Johannes was the first one to speak.

"What will they do to him?"

"They'll probably lock him up now and bring him to trial later," Douwe answered. "Maybe they just took him in for questioning. He might come home later," he added.

Johannes nodded. He left the stable to see in which direction the Black Partisans were taking his father. In the pit of his stomach he felt that his father wasn't just taken for questioning. Not if he had been correct in recognizing Willem's laugh. He scanned the road in front of the farm, but could see no one. He looked back at the farm building and ran behind the barn. In the distance, he saw the group of men walking along the canal towards the village.

Slowly Johannes trudged back to the stable. The excitement the Canadian soldiers had brought earlier that afternoon was gone. In silence, the three men finished their milking chores.

"You'd better tell your mother, Johannes," Douwe said.

Johannes stopped. He hadn't even thought about his mother. Too caught up in his own feelings, he'd completely forgotten that the rest of his family didn't know what had happened. He quickly walked through the laundry room, hoping his mother would be alone — wishful thinking in a household with so many people. But the door to the kitchen suddenly opened and his mother stood there with a milk pitcher in her hand. Johannes noticed the light in her eyes. She seemed younger this afternoon. He stared at her blankly.

She smiled and handed him the pitcher. "What's wrong, Johannes? Don't tell me you are not happy the war is over. Or has it not sunk in yet?"

"Yes, Mother. I am. I mean, I am very happy this war is over, but . . . "

"I know you worry about your father. But let's not think about that today." Her face grew more serious. "We'll deal with it when the time comes. Tonight I want to enjoy the feeling of liberation."

It seemed so long ago since he had seen her like this — so happy. How was he going to tell her about Father?

"What's the matter, Johannes?" his mother frowned. She closed the door to the kitchen behind her. They were alone in the laundry room.

"It's Father," Johannes started. "They . . . they came and took him away."

"Who?" His mother grasped his shoulders, all colour draining from her face. "Who, Johannes? Who?" She shook him.

"They wore black armbands. One had the letters DOL on it."

His mother's eyes bored into his. "No! They are the wrong people to take him. They are fanatics!"

Johannes' heart beat in his throat.

"What did they do?" Her fingers dug into his flesh, but he didn't move.

"They just took him."

"They just took him," his mother repeated. "They couldn't wait another day." She let go of his shoulders. Her body slumped against the wall. "They didn't say how long or where they were going to take him?" She closed her eyes.

"No." Johannes wasn't going to tell her what the last man had said, or that he suspected the men had been drinking. "It happened so fast, Mother. We were milking, then without any warning they came into the stable with their guns. Five of them."

Slowly she pushed herself away from the wall. She opened her eyes. "We don't know what's happening to him, so let's not worry yet." A faint smile crossed her face. "I don't want the others to be too concerned, so let's just say he's been taken in for questioning."

"But you said they were the wrong people," Johannes said.

"Shh." His mother touched her lips. "Get some milk for me. I'll tell the rest of the family." Then she opened the door to the kitchen and walked in.

Johannes stood rooted on the spot. The wrong people, she had said.

Even Grandfather didn't say much during their evening meal. Too many things had happened in one day. Johannes watched his mother. Composed, her own plate left untouched, she made sure everybody at the table had enough to eat.

The baby made cooing sounds and Sjakie and Sjors asked when they could go home.

"Soon," Maria said. "As soon as we can travel."

After clearing the table, Mother tugged Johannes' sleeve and nodded in the direction of the door. Without a word, he followed her into the hall.

"You and I should go to the police station in the village," she whispered. "Maybe we can find out where they've taken your father."

Johannes nodded and grabbed his jacket. "Wouldn't you rather have Grandfather come with you?" he said. After all, he was her father.

"No," she said. "I want you to come with me."

They took their bikes and in silence they rode into town. Johannes remembered the last time he'd biked into this village. It had been with Sietske when they had raided the distribution office. Then an image came to him, the image of a man jumping him from behind, to test him. Johannes shook off the memory and tried to focus on the things to come.

In the village, the streets were full of people. Johannes and his mother manoeuvred their bikes through groups of dancing and singing men, women and children. In the schoolyard stood two Canadian tanks. Young girls laughed with the soldiers and smoked cigarettes.

They pedalled down Main Street, right up to the police station. A small crowd had gathered in front. Something must have happened, Johannes thought. They stopped and left their bikes against the wall. Heads turned and people moved away. His mother rang the bell. An older police officer opened the door.

"What can I do for you?" he asked.

His mother looked at the crowd. "May my son and I come in?"

"Certainly, follow me." The officer let them in and closed the door behind them. They followed him down the hallway.

"My office is right in here," he said, as he opened a door. At the end of the hall Johannes saw, on a stretcher, a body concealed by a black sheet. As he closed the door behind him, he wondered if it was one of the last German soldiers who hadn't escaped in time. That would explain the crowd outside.

"Sit down." The officer waved to the two chairs in front of his desk.

"My name is Nynke van der Meer, and this is my son, Johannes," his mother said. She sat up straight and smoothed her skirt with the back of her hand.

The officer sat down and grabbed the sides of his chair. He blinked several times. "Ahem. Yes. You are Mrs. van der Meer who lives on the farm east of the bridge?"

"Yes," Mother nodded. "Five resistance members came to pick up my husband this afternoon and I wondered if you could give me some information regarding where they might have taken him."

Johannes saw the officer shift uncomfortably in his chair. "Yes," he said. "I can give you some information. Can . . . can I offer you a glass of water?"

"No, thank you. Just information, please."

Johannes felt uneasy. He didn't think the information would be good. His mother looked intently at the officer.

"Things got out of hand," the officer said, rubbing his hands together. "I think . . . I think those men had been drinking."

"Who?" Mother stood up.

"Please sit down, Mrs. van der Meer."

Slowly she sank back down in the chair. Her face had lost its colour. Johannes' mind went blank. All he could think of were the words, "Things got out of hand."

"How much did things get out of hand, Officer?" Mother's voice sounded restrained.

The officer stood up. Tiny drops of perspiration beaded his forehead. He walked over to the window. "They took the law into their own hands."

A tight cry escaped his mother's throat. Johannes' blood turned to ice. The body in the hall. The body in the hall was his father.

"He is here, Mrs. van der Meer. If you are ready, you will follow me. I would like you to identify him."

In a trance, Johannes stood up. He touched his mother's arm. Slowly she rose from the chair. The police officer came around his desk and opened the door. Johannes and his mother followed him down to the end of the hallway.

The last rays of sunlight passed through the small window above the front door. The policeman glanced at them as they stood in front of the covered body. Johannes felt the pressure of his mother's arm. The officer lifted the sheet.

His mother swayed. Johannes moved his arm under her elbow. He looked at the face in front of him. Bile rose from his throat into his mouth. He swallowed. And again. He concentrated on the face in front of him. His father's face. The high forehead, straight nose and lips pressed into a thin line.

A dried trickle of blood ran from a wound at his temple all the way down to his neck.

Executed. Just like that. No trial.

"Is this your husband, Mrs. van der Meer?" The officer looked at Mother.

She moved her lips, but no sound came. She nodded her head.

The officer lowered his voice. "You'd better go home now. I'll come by later," he said, as he walked them to the door.

Later, Johannes couldn't remember how they had made it home. He barely heard the murmur of the crowd outside the police station, or the sounds of the people dancing and singing in the streets.

The family sat around the table listening to Mother's distant voice. It seemed as if she was talking about somebody else, Johannes thought. Anneke was the most upset. She cried for a long time, her whole body shaking while Grandmother held her.

"No trial. He didn't even get a fair trial!" Grandfather shouted.

Pierre and Maria had no words. Maria cried softly while Pierre stared out the window.

As he had promised, the police officer arrived later that evening. He talked about people getting overexcited and drinking too much. Mr. van der Meer had become a victim of their excesses. The official called it revenge by a group of fanatics who thought they could take the law into their own hands.

They had shot him in a field just outside the town. At least the police had carried him into the station. The Germans would have left him at the place of execution. People executed by the Nazis were not allowed to be moved for twenty-four hours.

Mother told the officer that she would make funeral arrangements the next day. His father's body would be kept in the funeral home beside the church until the service. "The funeral will be the day after tomorrow," she said.

As she walked the officer to the door, she asked, "Do you have any idea who these men were? Can you find out for me, Officer?"

"No. That would be difficult, Mrs. van der Meer. They were wearing masks. I don't think we can find out who they were."

"You can't or you won't?" Mother asked.

The officer left. The question remained unanswered.

Later that night, Johannes walked over to Sietske's farm. He met her father outside, sitting on a tree stump.

"Johannes! Sietske is inside," Mr. Dijkstra greeted him. Johannes sat down beside him. "You're not out celebrating? She was expecting you earlier tonight."

"I . . . I came to say that they executed Father today. The funeral is the day after tomorrow." Johannes stood up and walked back the way he'd come.

"Johannes! Wait!" Mr. Dijkstra called.

But Johannes didn't look back.

The following day went by in a daze. All he could think of was the work that had to be done now that his father was gone.

That morning Johannes biked into Leeuwarden to notify Grandmother van der Meer. On the way, he met more Canadian tanks and jeeps. Although it was still early, people were singing and dancing in the streets. The red, white and blue flags, which had been hidden for five years, hung out of every window. The bright sun and blue sky added to the festivities.

But Johannes hardly noticed the excitement as he pressed the bell of the two-story home in the centre of the city. His grandmother, dressed in a faded black skirt and blouse, opened the door. She was in shock. After she calmed down a little, she told him that Uncle Jan had been captured by the *NBS*, the Dutch Interior Armed Forces. He had been locked up in an old school building with several other collaborators.

In the evening, Mother's sister Alie, who lived in Harlingen, sent a note. She didn't wish to attend the funeral of a traitor. Johannes passed the note on to his mother. She read it, then without a word crumpled the sheet of paper and threw it in the wastebasket.

The funeral was held the next day at two in the afternoon. Together, Johannes, his grandparents, Mother, Anneke, Pierre and Douwe biked silently into the village. They met the minister at the gate of the cemetery. Grandmother van der Meer had arrived early. Shivering in her old black coat, she sat on a wooden bench and dabbed her eyes with a white handkerchief.

Later, they all gathered around the grave. Johannes noticed the deep lines in his mother's face. Her old, navy coat hung loosely around her body. She stood straight, her shoulders squared.

Before the minister had a chance to speak, a young man on his bike stopped at the gate and yelled, "Durk van der Meer got what he deserved!" Then, laughing, he rode away. The harsh words echoed off the thick walls of the church. Johannes felt his mother cringe.

A cool April breeze encircled the small group of mourners. Johannes tried to concentrate on the minister's words, but the speech just washed over him. It felt as if he wasn't really there. This was all happening to someone else, not him.

The ceremony lasted about ten minutes. Quietly, everyone left. Anneke came and stood beside him, her warm hand seeking his cold one.

Outside the gate stood Sietske. He was surprised to see her. He hadn't expected her, a member of the resistance, to attend the funeral of a Nazi collaborator. She wore a navy blue skirt and a brown jacket. Her windblown curls framed her pale face. She hugged his mother and walked over to Johannes. He felt her arms around his neck, her tears on his face.

"I'll always be there, Johannes," she whispered.

With his one free arm, he pulled her close. For a moment he pressed his face against her curly hair; then she turned away and left.

Anneke let go of his hand and ran to be with her mother and both grandmothers. Alone, Johannes leaned against the gate of the cemetery. He watched his family gather up their bikes and leave.

Grandfather looked over his shoulder at Johannes. "Are you coming? The cows need to be milked."

Johannes nodded. Slowly, he retraced his steps to his father's grave. That morning Anneke had made a bouquet of wildflowers, which now lay on the casket. Their scent created a sour taste in his mouth.

Footsteps on the gravel made him turn. "Minne," he said softly.

Johannes hadn't seen Minne since the night of the prison raid. His curly hair had grown too long. His face was thinner and his pants didn't reach his ankles. Johannes tried to read his face. Minne returned the look, then lowered his eyes. He swallowed several times.

The anger welled up inside Johannes. He clenched his teeth and said in a bitter voice, "You got your wish, Minne. My father the collaborator is dead. Are you satisfied?"

Minne said nothing. He glared back at Johannes.

Slowly, Johannes, his head bent, his arms limp beside his body, turned and walked down the path to the gate of the cemetery.

"Johannes!"

Johannes halted.

"Johannes, I . . ." A choked cry escaped Minne's lips. Johannes turned. Minne, his face twisted in pain, walked towards him.

Johannes waited, his hands balled into fists.

Slowly, Minne placed both hands on Johannes' shoulders.

"Johannes," he said in a thick voice, "I never thanked you for . . . for saving me."

Johannes shrugged. "You would have done the same for me."

Tears filling his eyes, Minne held on to him. Johannes stood motionless. "And about your father." Minne controlled himself. "We both lost our fathers."

"Yes," Johannes nodded. "Yours died a hero. Mine was murdered as a traitor."

He pulled away from Minne and ran out of the church yard. Grabbing his bike, he looked back at his friend. He opened his mouth, but the words didn't come.

Johannes didn't hear the music in the streets as he headed home to milk the cows. In the days that followed, he buried himself in the work that awaited him at the farm.

# May 1945

The evening sun set, a red ball of fire full of promises for tomorrow. One by one, the large bodies of his father's cows settled down for the night. Johannes watched as the mist rose from the ditches in smoky lines. He planted his feet on the second bar of the gate. The quietness of the evening soothed him.

"Peace," he sighed. At peace, alone with nature. During the day there was none. Work had to be done. His grandfather ordered him around every minute. Even during dinner, Grandfather talked about the extra chores that could be done when Johannes had time. The last four weeks had been slowly suffocating him.

Grandmother was more reclusive since Father's death. It seemed as if she lived in another world.

Mother worked harder than ever, helping out with the farm work wherever she could and looking after her parents. Her clothes couldn't quite conceal the thinness of her body. Johannes wished his grandparents would go home, but every time he brought it up, Grandfather insisted they were needed here. Someone had to run the farm, and it would be in the best interests of everyone if they stayed. For how long? Johannes wondered. He never asked that question.

He sighed again. These living arrangements didn't work. Not for him.

The evacuees had left the week after the funeral. They couldn't wait to get home, even without knowing what was left of it. Pierre and Maria thanked the family and promised to write, but they hadn't been heard from since. They must have had better things to do than write letters. He imagined it would take them a long time to rebuild their home.

Anneke had gone back to school and soon found a friend whose father had been a member of the party as well. Her father was awaiting his trial. Anneke seemed to get over all the events more quickly than anyone else.

Father was never mentioned anymore. Grandfather had decided it was best to get on with life and forget the war as quickly as possible. "And work is the best medicine to heal wounds," he had added.

Johannes shook his head. He needed to get some sleep, but he wanted to treasure the silence for a few more minutes. He stared at the misty world around him. Birds settled down for the night, their chirping and whistling a mere lullaby. In the distance he heard the *who-who* of an owl. A whiff of burned grass teased his nostrils.

"I thought I'd find you here." Startled, he turned and saw his mother coming down the path to the gate.

"I didn't hear you," Johannes said.

"I didn't mean to disturb you."

Johannes reached for her hand as she climbed up to sit beside him.

"This is where you find what I've been looking for," she said. Johannes nodded, "Peace."

"I talked to Aunt Saakje tonight on the telephone. Uncle

Jan has been sentenced to one year in prison camp."

"One year?" Johannes said. "That doesn't seem very long. A year is gone before you know it."

"Yes," Mother agreed.

"If Father had gotten a fair trial, would he . . ." Johannes couldn't finish.

"A year, maybe two."

They sat, each with their own thoughts.

"I have been thinking, Johannes," his mother began. "Do you think you and I can run the farm together?"

Johannes turned to look at her. "Yes! Do you mean that?"

"Of course, I mean it. It's time we became independent. There is a drawback, of course. You can't go back to school."

"Yes. Of course not. I mean, I don't need to go back to school. I can always take evening courses later." He jumped down and stood beside the gate.

"We have to hire another hand. Douwe is getting older," Mother continued.

Johannes leaned against the gate, his chin resting on the bar.

"I know someone who's interested," she said. "He's a hard worker and reliable."

Johannes watched his mother's face in the fading light. She must have done a lot of thinking about this. "Who is it?" he asked.

"Minne," she smiled.

"Minne?" he repeated.

"You think you and Minne can work together?"

Johannes was silent. Even though Minne had come to see him after his father's funeral, they hadn't had any contact since. He and Minne had gone through too much — they couldn't be friends the way they used to be. But they could start all over and take it from there.

He felt a heavy weight lifting from his shoulders as he said, "We can both try. How will you tell Grandfather?"

"I don't know yet, but I'll do it first thing tomorrow morning."

A red glow in the western sky marked the sundown. Johannes gazed at the acres of land in front of him. It was all his. His, and one day . . . his and Sietske's.

"Your father loved being out here on evenings like this," Mother said in a soft voice.

Johannes shivered. He wasn't sure he wanted to talk about his father now.

"I know how you feel about him, Johannes," she said. "But I hope one day you will replace the resentment and hate with good memories."

Johannes swallowed.

"I know you have many questions, and so do I. For some of our questions, we will never find answers." She stopped and brushed aside a lock of her hair.

Johannes nodded. "Why did he stay with the Nazis till the end?" he asked thickly.

"I don't know, Johannes. He kept everything involving the party to himself."

"What did he do besides interpreting and organizing cattle transports for the enemy?" Johannes' voice rose. "What was so terrible that he needed to die?"

Mother shook her head. She looked out over the land, her eyes seeing nothing. "Who murdered him?" she whispered.

He held on to the bar of the gate. His knuckles turned white.

"I hope one day you will remember how he taught you to skate." In the distance a cow mooed. "He taught you how to find a plover's nest. He played hide and seek with you and Anneke." She waited. He sensed her tears.

She wiped her eyes, then, inhaling the evening air deeply, she said, "He was proud of you, Johannes. Especially when he found out you had been part of the group who freed the prisoners."

A cry escaped his throat. "He knew?" His voice wavered.

"Yes, Johannes, he knew."

Johannes swallowed several times. His chest filled with pain.

"He chose the wrong side during a time when it wasn't always clear if black was black and white was white, especially at the beginning of the war." Mother sighed and climbed down from the gate.

She placed her arm around his shoulders. "He was a good man, Johannes. He was a good man." Her fingers dug into his flesh before letting her arm drop away. She turned and walked back towards the house.

Slowly, his lungs released the trapped air. Johannes shuddered and collapsed against the gate. His eyes filled with tears, overflowed into rivers running down his face.

When darkness blanketed the land and the last tears were dry, he slowly retraced his mother's steps back to their home.

# Historical Note

Although this is a work of fiction, the events described are based on historical fact. Johannes, Minne, Sietske and their families are all the product of the author's imagination. The raid at the House of Detention in Leeuwarden actually happened, although in reality it involved many more people than depicted here.

These are some of the facts surrounding events depicted in the story:

In the early morning of May 10, 1940, German troops invaded the Netherlands. After five days of heavy fighting, the Dutch army was forced to surrender.

During the fall of 1942, church bells were plundered and taken to Germany from every town and village in Friesland.

In May of the following year, the Dutch people were ordered to hand over their radios and were forbidden to listen to illegal broadcasts.

During an air raid on the night of September 16, 1944, five Pathfinder-Mosquitoes and forty-eight Lancaster bombers dropped 960 bombs, destroying the air base of Leeuwarden.

The Dutch resistance conducted many successful raids at police stations, distribution centres and registrars' offices during the last year of the war. But the most spectacular raid happened on December 8, 1944, at the House of Detention in Leeuwarden, Friesland's capital. Fifty political prisoners were freed entirely without bloodshed. All fifty prisoners found a safe hiding place until the end of the war. After the raid, the German army commander wanted to conduct a house-to-house search of the city, but as he didn't have enough troops and couldn't get the support of the air base commander, it never happened.

The winter of 1944-1945, "the winter of hunger," was the coldest winter of the war. In the city of Amsterdam alone, 10,000 people died from starvation. Many people travelled into the country in search of food. However, even if they were successful, the German soldiers often took the food from them before they could return home.

The province of Friesland became a haven for "divers," people who needed to hide below the surface of society for fear of German persecution.

In February 1945, thousands of evacuees from the southern part of the Netherlands were sent to the northern provinces, where the people still had food and fuel supplies.

Montgomery's British army crossed the Rhine at Wezel on March 24, 1945. As a result of this action, the First Canadian Army under General Harry D.G. Crerar was able to liberate the northern part of the Netherlands.

On April 15, 1945, at 12:23 a.m., the first Canadian tanks entered Leeuwarden.

The many farmers and other citizens who belonged to the National Socialist Movement and collaborated with the Germans during the war were detained in prison camps. Some were sentenced to one to three years in prison, depending on the activities they had participated in during the war.

# Bibliography

Gunston, Bill. *Aircraft of World War 2* Octopus Books Limited, London, 1980.

de Jong, Dr. L. *De Overval* [The Raid] Em. Querido's Uitgeverij n.v., Amsterdam, 1962.

van Kampen, L. Mulder, J.J. Reitsma, C. van der Veer, J.J. *Friesland 1940-1945* Pers Boekerij b.v., Drachten/Leeuwarden, 1989.

Miller, Russell and the editors of Time Life Books. *The Resistance* Canada, 1979.

Posthuma, Eliza. *Under Frjemd Folk* [Under Strange People] Fryske Utjowerij "De Terp," Leeuwarden, 1979.

Wadman, Anne. *De fearren fan de Wikel* [The feathers of the hawk] Utjowerij Wimpel, Amsterdam, 1990.

Wadman, Anne. *De Unbitelle Rekken* [The Unpaid Bill] Stichting it Fryske Boek, Grou, 1992.

Wassenaar, Jaitsche. *It Pak Fan Us Heit* [My Father's Suit] Algemiene Fryske Underrjocht Kommisje, de Provinsje Frieslan, Ljouwert, 1993

# Pronunciation Guide

| | |
|---|---|
| Johannes | Yo-hann-es |
| Anneke | Ann-e-ke |
| Minne | Minn-e |
| Sietske | Seets-ke |
| Bauke | Bow-ke |
| Klaas | Klass |
| Willem | Vill-um |
| Jan | Yon |
| Piet | Peet |
| Nynke | Ning-ke |
| Durk | Dirk |
| Douwe | Dow-e |
| Saakje | Sak-ye |
| Jelle | Yell-e |
| Kees | Kase |
| van der Meer | van der Mare |
| Dijkstra | Dyke-straw |
| Friesland | Frees-land |
| Leeuwarden | Lay-oo-varden |
| Franeker | Fran-e-ker |
| Harlingen | Har-ling-en |
| Sjakie | Sha-key |
| Sjors | Shors |
| Pytsje | Peet-sje |
| Bijke | By-ke |
| de Jong | de Young |
| de Boer | de Bo-er |
| Jannie | Yonny |